BOSS UNDERCOVER

PART 3

J.S. BADHAM

Boss Undercover: Part 3

Copyright © 2019 by J.S. Badham.
All rights reserved.
First Print Edition: November 2019

Limitless Publishing, LLC
Kailua, HI 96734
www.limitlesspublishing.com

Formatting: Limitless Publishing

ISBN-13: 978-1-64034-794-6

Dedication

There are several people I would like to dedicate this book to.

First off, I would like to dedicate this book to my loving family. Thank you for always believing in me. Your support means more than anything. I really appreciate what've you done and what you continue to do to support me.

To Daniella. Thank you. I can't express how much your friendship means to be. I would be here for days. It would be longer than a dissertation.

Robbie, thank you. Honestly, I'm so glad I've met you. You're just awesome! Thank you for just being there and again supporting me constantly!

I would then like to dedicate this book to the reader. I want you to know that you should never give up on your dreams. Go for them! Let your story be known. Let your voice shine.

I hope you enjoy!

CHAPTER ONE

CLAIRE

Two weeks. She was dumbfounded, miserable, and worried. Her suspension at work had come as a total surprise. A *surprise* that was completely the opposite of pleasant. If Jonas's passing and Darren's shattered soul hadn't already dampened her spirits, then being placed under scrutiny from work had just about crushed it.

But there was *Zack.* At least with his efforts he'd managed to keep her sane and could muster a smile or two. He had been more than supportive; his constant reassurance had settled her incessant apprehension for most of the days. She didn't know what she would have done without him. Being stuck at the apartment all day or sluggishly moving around shop floors in an attempt for a fulfilling purpose meant her

1

morality was low until Zack came back into the picture. Their evenings spent together had become like a ritual. He would walk in from work, embrace her within his arms, and they'd sit on the couch sharing old anecdotes. She'd ask him about his day, and he would respond by comforting her on her speculation of work. She couldn't have asked for more. But it couldn't completely banish the fear of her losing her job. The mystery of why she faced disciplinary action was a heckling thought she couldn't seem to escape from. *What had she done? Why? How? Or even, who?* There had to be a good explanation for all of this. Possibly they had gotten her mixed up with someone else. Maybe it was a mistake. *Or* someone had it out for her. Either way, her fate would be settled Tuesday, the nineteenth of October. And that *was tomorrow*.

Zack had his arms wrapped around her shoulders as she sat between his legs, her head resting into the crevice of his neck. They had been watching some film on the television, and the adverts had just sprung up at this point. It was some car advertisement trying to entice viewers into the reality of purchasing its latest edition. The sound was just background noise compared to the clatter of fear ringing in Claire's head.

She sighed, squeezing Zack's hand that was entwined with her own.

"You okay?" he asked.

"Just nervous about tomorrow," she replied truthfully, turning her face into his shirt collar and inhaling the intense, delicious scent of his cologne. It was just enough to soothe some of her nerves temporarily.

"Don't be," he encouraged. "I'm sure they've got it all wrong. They've *got* to. Besides, we've been over this. What could you have done? Nothing. You know it. I know it. Heck, even Darren told you he knows it. It's just some cock-up on their end. I'm sure of it, *baby.*"

Claire's lips turned upwards a little. "*God,* you always know what to say. I'm sorry I've been moping about these last two weeks. I should have been trying to keep on my toes, keep positive. And *besides*, my brother's wedding is just around the corner. I should be looking forward to that."

"Don't apologise. You have *nothing* to apologise for." His tone was earnest and completely empathetic towards her situation.

Claire couldn't express how much she had fallen for this guy. These past two weeks had been more than enough to hint at a possible future in the long-term between them both. She couldn't imagine anyone else she would rather spend her evenings and days with. It was possible that she had fallen more than what could be perceived. *Was that possible? To fall more in love?*

She sat a little up more and turned her body towards him so her bottom rested on his left thigh. Her projection of fear had diminished little by little as lust replaced it. Her fingers swept across his jaw. "Kiss me, Zack," she muttered, demanding his attention. They hadn't had sex since last week. Something else, she felt, had been snatched from the misery of her predicament.

He complied, leaning in as he slowly pressed his lips softly to hers. The contact sparked a fervent hunger within the tips of Claire's toes that her lips became demandingly needy. Her tongue slid beneath his whilst his hands ran around to tighten their grip across her back as he brought her closer in.

Claire swiveled her hips within his lap, clawing her fingers through his thick, black hair, and felt herself drifting on cloud nine as his lips teased behind her ear and then trailed towards her neck. She was desirably hungry, as was he, his hands sliding up her shirt before cupping her breasts. A gasp left her lips as she felt overwhelmed, longing for *him* to be inside of her. Hastily, her hands unbuckled his belt, the zipper on his trousers wanting to free him. Zack took charge as he lifted her up; her legs hooked around his as he carried her towards her bedroom.

He laid her down on the bed, stripping her top from her torso and then unhooking her bra.

Claire shivered in delight at the sensation of his lips sucking on her hardened nipples. Her body felt re-animated.

"You're…so beautiful," he spoke huskily in between kissing her breasts. She couldn't help but blush. And she couldn't help how much she needed him. Claire tore open his shirt, breaking buttons as they flew off in odd directions. Zack chuckled darkly before he kissed her lips possessively and then proceeded to strip off her jeans and then her knickers. Then his jeans and boxers came off, and before she knew it, he entered her. Their bodies rocked together, their breathless voices draining from the exhilaration of their spirits connecting *intimately*. Zack picked up the pace, moving his hip bones harder into her, feeling her inside walls throb at the build-up.

"*Fuck,*" she heard him grunt, quickening more as she begged him on, her pleas not silencing until it happened. She felt it rush from her. And then he released inside, collapsing only a little upon her before he rolled on to the left side of her bed. Claire was breathless but hungry for more. She didn't need to ask as she climbed on top of him and worked her hips in motion as his fingers kneaded into her ass.

***

ZACK

"Well, this is killing two birds with one stone. Both my least favourite people here sharing a classic pint of beer and bowl of peanuts. Charming," Zack remarked. Kyle sat on the one side of the booth and Jared adjacent to Zack. It was half ten. It'd been an hour since his hot rendezvous with Claire. Adrenaline was still pumping through his veins. Claire had fallen asleep shortly after, then he snuck out quietly and headed into town.

Kyle thrust up his bottle of beer. "Anytime, my man." Then he exhaled with a bizarre sound exiting his mouth as he added, "Ah, God. Life, ay? Your company is in jeopardy, you're *actually* dating, and so far, you're winning the lousy bet."

He licked his bottom lip as he grinned.

"Thanks for the reminder. And we both know that this deal was just not practical," Zack replied as he rolled his eyes.

Kyle nodded with agreement then punched his index finger on the table as he asserted, "Yeah, I know. It didn't really have the foundations. But it would be fucking gold if you'd just lead on Trevor for a joke."

Jared chuckled, clasping hands with Kyle as a means of a handshake. "Damn, Kyle. That would be gold."

Zack tapped the bottom of his bottle

persistently as he requested their silence. "Will you guys knock it down a peg? I came to drink my misery, not listen to you idiots badger on."

Kyle held up in his hands in surrender as he chuckled. *"Okay. Okay."*

"Anyway," Jared interjected, leaning over the table a little as he directed his question towards his brother. "So, what is the sex like?"

"Jared," Zack scolded as he punched his brother in the right arm due to the appearance of a waitress passing by the table doing her rounds. "God, you're fucking annoying," Zack added with distaste, ignoring his brother's slight wincing.

Kyle smirked. "Well. Our Zacky also said he loved her. Isn't that right?" Zack disregarded the comment and rolled his eyes, once again pushing the bottle towards his lip to swallow another mouthful of sweet alcohol instead. "What is that like, anyway?" Kyle prodded him.

Zack scoffed. "You're making it seem like it's a fucking science experiment."

"Took you long enough, though," Kyle argued with a smug expression still painted on his lips.

Zack had to give him one, considering that it did take almost a gazillion years to figure out that he had feelings. "Yeah, *well*." He exhaled as he leant further back in the plush back of the booth.

"You know it's changed you," Kyle began,

his eyes narrowing into tiny slits as he debated over his initial comment. "I think it *has*. You're softer. Like a...teddy bear! You used to not give a fuck but now...well, it's a good change, I suppose. Won't be the same now going out to nightclubs with you. The VIP section will look dry as fuck in your corner while me and your brother are having lovely ladies scooting up further onto our laps."

"I hadn't thought of that, but yeah," Jared agreed, tuning in to the conversation. "Also, what about Mother? You know she had her heart set on her friend's daughter? Nicola, wasn't it? Although I suspect you won't get much there cause she's lesbian. I heard she hooked up with some girl at an engagement party. So, you gonna tell Mother when this all goes over?"

"Yeah, Nicola. We're both aware of our mothers sniffling their noses into setting something up between us. And you know I've told Mother countless times that she can't get involved with that part of my life, so it's nothing to even be concerned about. But then, that's my second problem. I still haven't told Claire who I really am. I mean...*of course* I'm not pretending not to be myself. I'm still *me*. I just don't wear a name tag addressing me as CEO of the company." Zack finished with a train of sighs as he twirled the bottle of beer between his fingers casually.

"Yeah, *you're fucked*." Kyle inhaled.

"Yeah, sorry, man," Jared agreed.

"*Jeez*, thanks. I know I can trust on you two morons to have my back," Zack sneered as he rolled his eyes for the third time. "I also don't think you realise the predicament I'm facing with Claire mysteriously being suspended at work. I know it's got something to do with those emails. That *traitor* within my company. And if it is, it's all my fault. Somehow, I've got her involved. I can't be sure until tomorrow. The board hadn't even announced to me about her suspension until today."

"To answer both, I think you should just come forward. Tell Claire who you *really* are and fire that employee *now*. And then job done. Just get it off your chest now," Kyle suggested before picking up a peanut from the bowl and plopping it on his tongue.

"Yeah, that sounds like a *piece of cake*. But then I'll never find out who's ordering my employee to sniff out the company. I *need* to know who is playing puppeteer. And…there's another predicament. I'm going to a wedding ceremony—"

"Wait, are you getting married?" Jared exclaimed, his brows in competition as to which one could get to the centre of his forehead the quickest.

"No!" Zack hissed, smacking the back of his brother's head lightly. "How am I related to you sometimes? *Sheesh*," he groaned. "Her brother's getting married this month, and if I *remember*, in literally one and half weeks."

Jared was still wincing.

"Well, tell her *now*," Kyle said, shrugging his shoulders. "I mean, it'll save you all the hassle, and it will look better than after all that, because, my friend, that's a big commitment. You're literally making yourself known to the family. Like you're literally fucking your big toe in and out with the possibility of future commitment with your girl. And I mean fucking—"

"Kyle, *I get the picture*," Zack cut in, silencing Kyle. "But I can't. I have to focus on the company. That's a priority—" Then he grabbed a couple of peanuts and shoved them in his mouth.

"And she isn't?" Jared inputted after nursing the sore area across the back of his head.

"*Of course,* she is. I just can't. Not right yet. I have a couple of weeks before the publication of the magazine. And that means time to find out who's behind those emails and hopefully get my projects back on track. Then…I'll tell her," Zack replied.

Jared shrugged his shoulders. "*Well,* you better get cracking. I mean, what's the worst that could happen when you do tell her?"

"*Death*." Zack froze.

***

CLAIRE

Claire had seen the note on her bedside table. Zack had gone out for an hour. She found herself now unable to sleep. It was half eleven. She had approximately eleven hours till judgment day. And *now* the nagging thoughts of fear and angst were taking residence again in the pits of her mind. There was no point trying to force herself to sleep. It would be useless. All night she would have temporary insomnia.

Instead, she decided to give Darren a call, wondering how he was doing. As much as she was allowed to be scared for the security of her job, Darren's actual loss was more derailing than her own. She swiped open her phone as she pinpointed his number and sat up, covers draping across her naked body, listening to the echo of rings. She wasn't sure he was going to pick up until seventh ring. "*Hey,* I'm just ringing to check up on you. And…*selfishly*, I need a friend right now," she announced, anxiously squeezing her mobile tightly as she anticipated his response. They hadn't spoken since the first week she'd gotten the email. He had told her how he felt before asking politely if he could spend a week or so without a phone call. It seemed more than overdue, and Claire missed him terribly.

Darren coughed a little before he spoke, his usual energetic voice dead, replaced with a guttural whisper that only made Claire's heart ache with pain. "I'm okay, Claire. Just—well, tired and…how are you? It's your meeting tomorrow, isn't it?"

"*Yes.* I'm okay. I'm more concerned about you. Have you been eating? Drinking? Have you…gone out of the apartment yet?"

There was a pause on the line. "*I'm* getting there. Let's not dwell on me—how are you *really* feeling, Claire?" he asked.

"*Truthfully,* I'm scared. I have no idea what they're going to pitch forward to me tomorrow. I've barely slept these past two weeks, and I feel like I won't get a blink tonight. I just don't understand why this is happening, but…Darren, you don't want to hear this. I'm being selfish coming to you with this when—"

"*Nonsense,* Claire. I'm actually glad you rang up. It helps hearing normality. I want to apologise for being distant the last week. I just *really* needed some space to—"

"I know. Don't apologise, Darren," Claire interjected. "I don't blame you for wanting space. How…did…" She paused intentionally, fearing the mention of Jonas's name would break him down.

Darren sighed a little. "I actually went through some of Jonas's old things that he left at my apartment. I found a list."

"What did it say?"

"Just about us, really. About our plans. *London,* stuff like that," Darren said quietly. "It just proved even more…how Jonas…really loved me. God." He stopped as he exhaled. "Hearing it said in past tense just doesn't feel right. He should be here, Claire, and I know I can't do anything to turn back time, but…*god,* would I do anything just to have him back." His tone was getting quieter by the second, and Claire blinked back tears. Darren sounded so dead. It just wasn't right hearing him sound so defeated, lifeless, and like a stranger. Even before she could get a word in, Darren pushed with another question directed towards her. "So, what about you and Zack?"

Claire held her breath as she attempted to shift away her threatening tears, knowing it would be selfish to cry when he was there on the other line, trying to so hard to keep a brave face on. After what seemed an eternity, she began, "We're doing fine. *Really.* I hate speaking about us when—"

"Claire, it's okay. I want to hear. Please," Darren interjected, no raise in his voice, still that equal dead tone. *It was so right*, a part of him had died when Jonas had gone.

Claire sniffled as she found courage to continue, "We're good. I mean—he's coming with me to my brother's wedding." Her tone piped up a little as she attempted to cut away the dismal atmosphere lingering between them both.

"That's great. He'll meet your family then," Darren said.

"Yeah, he…will. Darren, are you sure you don't need me to come over?"

"Claire, I'm okay. Just having this phone call is enough for me. I know you have my best interest at heart, babes. But I'm okay." Just hearing him call her that term of endearment, the one he'd always use day in and day out at work, reminded her just for a second that the old Darren was still there. Not lost. Not lost at sea. Just hidden.

"Okay."

"Claire, I'm going to go now. I need to continue sorting through…some of his stuff. I'll call you tomorrow after your meeting. Don't worry, I'm sure it's all a misunderstanding," Darren informed her, then they said their goodbyes before he ended the call. It made her want to cry; the strangle of breath and prickle of hairs across her skin just swarmed wasps of emotion all over her.

She was thankful when she heard the front door click open and then Zack entering the bedroom. He noticed how uneasy she appeared and immediately embraced her in his arms. "You okay?" he muttered against her hair as he sat down on the side of the bed.

"Yeah."

He smelt of alcohol upon his breath, and it began to entwine with the musky scent of his cologne, indulging all her female hormones into a raging fire. The intense feeling guided her closer towards him, like a silent word of whisper as she hung her arms around his neck. She studied his eyes, holding her breath as she felt his heart hammer against his ribcage. Claire threaded her fingers through his hair as she hungrily kissed his lips. He instantaneously responded with his hands comfortably resting on her hips. He'd only been gone an hour or so, and already her veins were filling with lust once again. Instead, she pulled back, choosing to position herself against his torso as he lay back and willingly accepted that tonight; she just wanted to be held close.

CHAPTER TWO

ZACK

Obviously, Zack felt terribly guilty. To think he had the power to turn things around for Claire but choosing instead to remain hidden by the shadows made him feel like a monster. After watching her pace the apartment floor endlessly upon the early hours of the morning, muttering words of encouragement to herself and trying not to have a mental breakdown, it was a wicked play how he obnoxiously pretended alongside, acting as if it wasn't, he who could end her misery. But as much as Claire was his priority, it was important that he ratted out the mole who was disrupting his projects for sustainability. So, if *per se* this meeting was her downfall, it would be something he'd be willing to sacrifice. *Even if the woman he had confessed he loved was falsely accused.*

Claire's hand squeezed Zack's one last time before her grip loosened and she headed off into the empty lift. He stood there on the outside, his heart hammering anxiously as the doors slid shut and she disappeared from sight. *There was no going back.*

Olivia had phoned him earlier to detail the meeting concerning an employee, aka Claire, attending in front of the board over high conspiracy charges against the company. It didn't take a genius to realise that they were referring to Graves' tango with the stranger upon his actions of detailing Zack's plans to Label Works for one, and the many others before that had failed. They just didn't know it was *him.* Instead, they were going to make the biggest mistake of their careers sending an innocent employee down for the responsibility of Graves, and that angered Zack. But there was nothing he could do until he sourced out the encrypted soul pulling the strings on Graves and potentially others within the company.

Zack pressed the button to call for the lift. As the CEO, he'd been invited to attend to the meeting, but under the circumstances, it wasn't possible, therefore he had asked if his presence could remain but through video call and without the picture. It wasn't questioned nor was *Zack Chase's* presence after Olivia had recorded his attendance to work as late due to a dentist appointment. *The convenience of dentist appointments.* Graves wouldn't be sniffling at his back.

The doors slid open, and he entered, pressing the number to highest floor. A few other souls joined him in the shaft as they took turns to jab in their floor numbers. *Soon, I won't be seen as invisible,* Zack thought. His eyes studied each employee discreetly. Each face would soon recognise Zack and reject their recognition of his father once the publicity was out. *But then a certain someone will know.* And how would that go down? Zack ignored the thought, knowing the answer to that already.

After, stopping more than several times, Zack finally reached *his* floor. Olivia was at her desk as he passed, quickly following him like a sheep as she waited accordingly for his instructions. The office looked like it had gained a bit of residence from the specks of dust growing on the surface of the desk, but other than that, it remained the same. He headed for his chair and opened his laptop, dashing the cursor quickly to Skype and ensuring the live video of himself sitting there wouldn't be projected within the board's room. It was ten, still another fifteen minutes until it started. He couldn't help but wonder how Claire must be feeling. *Scared? Anxious? Annoyed? Angry?* Not that he could blame her. Part of him wondered how Graves had convinced the board under the suspicions of conspiracy.

Olivia stood by, holding her notepad. "Mr. Benson, we have all the prominent members of the board attending except Mr. Johnson and Mrs. Oswald. They've had to answer to attend to another one of our establishments elsewhere. But," she flicked a page over, "the rest will be making a decision upon Miss Claire Winter, an employee within marketing and sales who has been suspended over conspiracy," she read aloud. "Sir, I don't mean to pry," she added, a hint of curiosity embedded within her tone. "But if we know Mr. Graves is our perpetrator, why are we not…pressing him instead?"

Zack swallowed, feeling sweat glisten on his forehead. It was a good question. But his intentions were also logical. "I want to black-mail Mr. Graves into revealing his accomplice. But to do that, I must have him think he is in the clear. Then I'll worm him in. And find out hopefully who he is working for. We have the emails that clearly put him at fault, but I want the other person. The one behind all of this," he explained honestly, knowing his wicked play was costing a valuable employee but also *his girlfriend.*

Olivia nodded. "I see. How do you plan on getting Mr. Graves to reveal his accomplice…*when* he doesn't know who this person is himself?"

Another good question. "I haven't *exactly*

19

decided that yet. I'm sort of running on a whim. But somehow, I'm going to have Mr. Graves rat him out for me. But for now, he thinks he's in the clear," Zack replied, feeling a little less confident.

Their attention was alerted to the incoming notification upon his screen. Zack accepted the Skype call, where it immediately transferred him to a live video of the meeting room. There were a few members of the board sitting around the long conference table, conferring in high discussion already. These were the judges of Claire's fate.

Someone at the head of the table began to address the group. He was a plump, short man dressed head to toe in a navy blue tailored suit. Each member quietened as they drew their complete attention like magnets towards him.

"Ladies and gentlemen, may I have your attention, please. Be aware that Mr. Benson will be listening in on this meeting today. But full powers will be granted to the board concerning our decision," the man said, the audio sounding like it was being projected from inside a can.

There was complete silence in the room. The man continued. *"It's the nineteenth of October two thousand and sixteen."* He glanced towards his wristwatch. *"The time is ten thirty-three. We call upon Miss Claire Winter."* Then he cleared his throat, walking across to his right and out of sight towards where Zack could only presume was the door.

The man returned, attending to his own unclaimed seat, whilst Claire slowly walked towards the head of the table and stood behind the empty chair. She resumed standing until some other voice ushered her to politely sit. She complied obediently. Zack felt sick to the core. Her facial features were enough to show him that she was scared like she just seen a ghost. This was completely unfair and cruel. But getting the information on whoever was manipulating Graves was just more important at this time. *She would get this all back.*

"Miss Winter, you've been called to the board upon inquest concerning evidence revealed two weeks ago relating to your inconspicuous motives towards damaging the company's investment that have now just been brought into light. Do you accept?" It was the same deep, gruff voice from the short, plump man who addressed Claire. As he had spoken, her face had completely turned pale. She was startled. Zack couldn't even begin to imagine what she was feeling. *What are they talking about? This makes no sense. I haven't done anything.* The countless questions he could only assume were piling up high. At any point, she could be on the brink of tears or filling with anger. He was not to know.

She seemed to remain steady as she

responded. *"I deny this accusation. I have no idea what I'm being accused of. My intentions for this company are nowhere near malicious. What evidence has been provided to the board to account me as the perpetrator?"*

Zack leaned in closer. He could almost sense Olivia edging closer as she stood by watching the laptop screen. There was a pause for four seconds or so until the same man who Zack was starting to believe was the main leading force of the board spoke in reply to her statement.

"Miss Winter, the evidence we've collected has numerous exchanges across email between yourself and some other who we believe to be outside contact, conspiring against the company. You've revealed and evidently manipulated data from previous projects before that seemed focused on Mr Benson's plans for sustainable homes. This all comes under your email address. Could you explain?"

One of the female members passed over a couple sheets of paper stapled together to which Zack could only presume was the fatal evidence that Graves must have issued to account Claire as responsible. Her eyes told it all. She looked gobsmacked, utterly cofounded. *This was hard to watch.*

"This—this isn't me. I-I never sent these emails," she objected, shaking her head as she flicked through the sheets, desperately trying to make sense of it all.

"This is *so* wrong," he heard Olivia mutter to herself. He couldn't have agreed with her more. It didn't even seem right intruding on the discussion.

"But Miss Winter, it's your *email. These were found in the server associated to your name, so we cannot even begin to suggest that they've been manipulated. So, what are you trying to say? Has someone else sent them from yours?"* the leading figure suggested. *"I mean, please."* He chuckled dryly, causing a few to stir and join in. *"The evidence is* right *there."*

Claire shook her head. *"But this isn't me. Someone must have. I have no intentions of disrupting the company. I fully supported these projects. I've put time and effort! I consistently smash targets. Why would I threaten my career for* this?*"*

"That's what we would like to know. After all, you're right. *Your record is good, so please enlighten the board, Miss Winter, why you decided to conspire. Who is this other contact you're conferring with? Do they work at another company? Why target specific projects?"* The man clasped his hands together. His authority oozed within his voice.

Claire frowned. *"It's not me! Please, I have no idea of this. These aren't mine. You have to believe me. I wouldn't do this!"* Her plea was useless; even Zack could see how the board ignored it like litter being carelessly discarded on a pavement. They had the evidence, evidence that was just too strong to be argued against. Zack wasn't surprised. Graves had done his work; his outside help had ensured that an innocent employee was about to be sent down.

But couldn't Zack do something? Couldn't he just speak? Save her? But the cost. The cost was far too great. It was killing him doing nothing, but his intentions had to stand for something.

"Miss Winter, I think we've heard enough. We appreciate your defence, but I think you need to accept your responsibility. Whatever motivated you clearly had gotten the best of you. As the board, we had to decide, a decision we already made even before this meeting. The evidence stands, you're to blame. So, as it stands, we're going to have to dismiss you, Miss Winter—"

"What? No, I-I didn't do anything," Claire interjected, fear drowning clearly within her face. Zack sighed as he rubbed his forehead, unable to watch any longer. He closed the laptop lid and sunk back into his chair.

Olivia was quiet.

"This is unacceptable, but for now, we must focus on drawing out this outside contact," he announced, knowing he was trying to justify his lack of support. There was only Olivia within the room. It seemed more appropriate to suggest he was addressing himself.

"Understood, sir. Is there anything else I can

do or can I be excused please?" she said quietly, looking down to her black flats.

Zack swallowed, nodding as he waved his hand to usher her permission. "Yes, you can. I shall be leaving in a second myself," he declared. She scuttled quickly out the room, leaving him alone.

***

CLAIRE

The board dismissed her. She was miserable as she left the room, her posture slouching as she sluggishly made advance to the wall opposite the room and began to rummage for her phone within her bag. *This couldn't be happening.* Fired. *None of this made sense. They weren't my emails. I never sent those.* But it was there printed black and white, physical evidence of a non-existent conversation she was accused of having with some other contact conspiring against the company.

Claire wanted to cry. She wanted to tear the place apart. She wanted to yell and scream and shout, but instead she chose to remain calm, watching as members of the board exited the room, chatting and displaying smug expressions, completely ignoring her presence. They were chuffed with themselves, unable to see that their actions were wrong. *I hadn't done anything,* she thought.

What about the bills? Food? How am I going to survive? What am I going to do now? I have no job. I've lost a friend; my best friend is practically dead from his loss, and now I have no financial stability. Claire was consumed with dread, utterly broken. All that waiting for two weeks and yet as the board had politely said, *They'd already decided my fate.* She wasn't sure what to do. All these emotions of anger, disbelief, and distress were burning through her veins. She didn't know what to with them.

Her hands shakily grasped her phone after digging it from beneath her purse. It was hard as she sought for Zack's number. She *needed* him more than ever.

He picked up on the second ring. "Claire? What happened? What did they say?"

Her voice trembled. "They've *dismissed* me, Zack. They've actually dismissed me. I just— just don't understand. They accused me of conspiring against the company. And they have these emails that have my email address associated to these messages. Like what the hell! *God, I have no job!"* Tears were threatening to brim within her eyes as she sunk down against the wall. Then she added quietly, "I'm coming down to the department to collect my things. Will you be there for me?"

"Of course."

Claire hung up, trying as best to stand up. She just couldn't understand any of this.

It didn't take long to return to the department. *The department* she could no longer call home. Each face engaged in their activity had no idea. *Not a single idea.* They didn't know this was her last day. Most of them probably wouldn't care.

She pushed the strap of her bag across her shoulder as she slowly trailed to her desk. Jason caught up to her side to ask her how she was. Claire lied to his face, smiled, and went on. It was too real if she told him the truth. She'd rather maintain the façade, pretend that everything was all right, than face reality.

As she expected, Zack sat at her desk, his hand cupping his chin as he intensely stared off into the distance. He seemed preoccupied but broke from his trance immediately when she dropped her bag onto the floor beside him. She was thankful that her cubicle blocked any prying eyes.

"Claire," he spoke softly, standing up as he embraced her within his arms. She wanted to choke tears, but strangely enough she kept strong, reeling her emotions far away as she tightened her grip around his torso. *It felt like home.* His lips kissed the top of her head.

"I'm *so* sorry," he muttered, rubbing his hand then across her back. "This is wrong."

Claire snorted as she pulled back. "Why are

you sorry for? Heck, it's not your fault." She sighed as she completely detached from him and took her seat. "I just don't understand. You believe me, don't you? I couldn't—"

"*Of course,* I do," he cut in. "I know that wasn't you. But what we should be thinking, who's planted this on you? Because someone must have."

Claire lifted her brows. "Is it bad I want to blame Monica?" Her short chuckle was dry and humourless as she began to collect her things from her desk. Zack was quiet behind her. She looked behind to see him narrowing his eyes to the left of the aisle at something or someone.

"What's up?" she asked curiously.

Zack shook his head. "I'm just annoyed for you." Then he squeezed her shoulders. "We'll fight this, Claire."

"*How?*" she said defeatedly. "What could I possibly do to change things now?" Claire exhaled, turning to face her desk as she continued to pack what she could manage into her handbag. "I've been *dismissed.* I have no job. I probably won't ever get another. They'll have this on my record as we speak. Face it, I'm done for."

His persistence was admirable, she had to admit. He was trying his best to reassure her. "Claire, don't give up. We'll figure something out. We'll fight this. Get a lawyer or—do *something.*"

Claire didn't reply.

"Miss Winter, *my office*," she heard the familiar old, raspy voice of Graves intruding into their space. Claire turned in her seat, watching as Graves stalked away.

"*Claire, don't,*" Zack warned.

"Why?"

"He's nothing but *trouble*. Let's just go. I'll come up with an excuse," he explained, sounding desperate for Claire to stray away from him.

"I should see what he has to say. Besides, maybe, it will be my chance to speak my mind. I'm a free woman, after all," she stated confidently, standing up and complying with Graves' order. "*I have nothing else to lose.*"

Graves was sitting at his desk when she entered. That sprout of confidence she felt suddenly died as she closed the door behind her. The reality was sinking in deeper. *She was fired. No job.* And her former boss was looking meaner than ever as he pulled a face of disappointment as she meekly stepped further into his cage.

"Miss Winter," he began. *They were even back on terms of formality.* "It's a *disappointment*, to say the least. My top employee within this department and you've *disgraced* us all by conspiring…but it's your *own* fault." He narrowed his eyes. "You can't do *anything* now."

29

"Mr. Graves, I have by no means done what I have been accused of. I can only say this, however: I'm glad I no longer have to be manipulated by you and Monica Andrews. I shall not miss the constant work you put on me. So, if that's all, I shall be leaving," she replied firmly.

Graves seemed to adopt suspicion within his eyes. *"You have no idea, do you?"* he muttered.

"What do you mean?"

He cleared his throat. *"That*—that I was *planning* on giving you the promotion instead," he spoke hastily, gesturing his hands forward as he lazily pointed at her. "But you have gone and done this. *So,* I'm sorry that you've been so foolish, Miss Winter."

"I'm not so sure I'm convinced about that, Mr. Graves. But if that is the case, I would have rejected it," she responded before dismissing herself without allowing another word.

CHAPTER THREE

ZACK

Claire had barely touched her food. Her fork was playing with the meatball rolling from one end of the plate to the mountain of mash on the right side. He intentionally cleared his throat, hoping to catch her attention, but she remained stubbornly stuck in a trance. *Not that he could blame her.* Her Tuesday had been *disastrous*.

"Claire, we'll work through this," he stated, reaching for her hand across the table. She looked up, offering a weak smile before turning back to her plate of food she continued to play with. "Are you not going to eat?"

She shook her head.

This *was* destroying him. He hated seeing her so lifeless and miserable. This isn't what he wanted nor intended. It should be Graves without the job. He should be paying the punishment. *Not Claire.*

"Claire, maybe I should be honest about—"

But he was cut off by the abrupt intrusion of her mobile ringing on the side of the table. He glanced at the screen—it was her mother calling. Claire seemed to sit up more as she edged her hand slowly towards the electronic device but was hesitant as to whether she wanted to respond to the beckoning call. After all, he could only imagine she was fearing admitting to her mother she had lost her job.

"Are you *not* going to answer it?"

Claire pressed her lips tightly together. She was contemplating over it. Another three rings and then she picked it up and slid her finger across the screen to answer. Zack remained quiet as he observed her communicate, trying her best to sound content than what she was really feeling.

"Hey, Mom. No, I'm okay," she replied, a clear lie as she slowly got up. Claire squeezed Zack's shoulder as she passed him before what he could assume was her needing space as she headed towards her bedroom.

Zack remained sitting there. *What was he going to do?* How on earth could he sort out this mess? *His mess.* For a moment, Zack knew he was going to confess until that phone call. Maybe it was selfish to have put another dilemma in Claire's court. Maybe he should be thankful for that call. To think he could have admitted to who he really was. Then what? Claire would just accept it and they'd live happily ever after? *Of course not.* It would be another punch in the face. Another problem weighing down on her shoulders.

But he *needed* to do something. *Anything.* To make things right at the cost of his company's sake.

He stood up and then placed Claire's dish in the microwave for safe-keeping before he headed out the kitchen towards her bedroom. On the other side of the door, he could hear her diving into her circumstance, admitting her job loss. Her voice was on the verge of crying at any point. Zack decided to quietly enter. She was startled by his presence, but it did not falter her attention to the phone.

"Yeah, I know. I know. I just don't understand—"

Zack sat on the left hand side of the bed before kicking his legs on and then encouraging her to nestle within his arms. She complied, resting her head against his bicep as she continued to converse and listen to whatever her mother had to say.

The conversation must have carried on for another fifteen minutes before Claire ended the call. She didn't say anything at first nor did he. Instead, they both chose to remain silent.

"I told her," Claire finally said. "She's angry at their decision. She said to me that we'll get through it like you've been saying. But…it doesn't make difference. *I'm still jobless."*

"But we will get through this," Zack reassured, rubbing his hand up and down her shoulder.

"Do you still want to go to my brother's wedding with me?" She changed subjects.

"Yes, of course. You know I said I will."

"*Good.*"

Zack bit his inner cheek. "*Claire.*" He paused. *No, he couldn't bring it up.* The time wasn't right. It just wouldn't be fair. "Just keep positive. I'm sure everything will get better."

It was difficult to pretend that everything was all right when it was far from. Zack wasn't even sure why he was still keeping this façade up. Claire had lost her job, he had no ideas on how to get Graves to rat out his mystery accomplice, and the failure of his projects were amounting to more pressure on his shoulders.

***

Claire had been desperately circling jobs ads in the morning newspaper, unable to comprehend that with an attached side note of conspiracy charged against her name, she pretty much had a narrow choice to who was willing to employ her. Any of the bigger companies with similar roles wouldn't even turn an eye to her. Zack knew that. Her employability record was tainted because of Graves and whoever he had hiding up his sleeve.

"At this point, I'll be lucky if I get a job. All of these will want a reference from my last employer. I'm just gonna have to find a small shop or something, find someone who will either turn a blind eye or not ask for my employability record," Claire explained, sounding fed up and frustrated as she folded the paper in half.

Zack was sitting opposite, quiet and shamefully guilty. This just wasn't fair. This shouldn't be happening. Claire didn't deserve this. This was all his fault. He shouldn't have stepped into her life. He'd brought all this onto her. And he knew it was only going to get worse once the truth finally slipped out.

"Shouldn't you be getting to work?" she inquired, looking up from her coffee mug and meeting his eyes.

Zack shook his head. "It—doesn't matter. I'm just going to stay home and make sure you're okay. I—"

"Zack, don't be silly. You can't not go to work because of *me,*" she interjected. "Besides…you're the breadwinner at this moment until I find another job. I have just enough to cover next month's rent and afford some…food." Claire groaned as she ran her hands through her hair. "God, I hate feeling so dependent. It just *sucks*."

"You'll find a job, Claire," he reassured, providing comfort to her hand across the table. His fingers caressed the soft pad of skin. "I'm sure of it." Doubts were nagging him as he sat back in his chair and slipped his hand away from hers. *Was everything going to be all right?* Could he promise that? And what if she knew that he literally had the authority to change things and prevented what shouldn't have happened but didn't because selfishly he was too concerned about his company and the outside contact sticking their noses in? Wouldn't that change things? Claire wouldn't look at him the same. She'd hate him.

"I'll be...fine." She exhaled. "Just—just don't worry about me and go to work. I don't want to be the reason for you losing your job," she said, trying to present a strong smile that was failing to convince Zack.

But he'd complied, knowing Claire was stubborn as a mule and would persist ceaselessly.

Maybe if he was lucky something would crop up.

At least that's what he hoped when he exited the lift shaft and stepped into the department. Zack was a little clueless to what to do. Looking around at the maze of cubicles, he was wondering why on earth he was bothering to keep up appearances down here. But what was he supposed to do upstairs? He'd made it transparent to Olivia that he clearly knew not what to do with the impending problem of Graves.

Why did I bother? I should have just listened to my father. This quest for sustainability was stupid. Even someone on the outside agrees. The thoughts swarmed his mind as he walked slowly towards Claire's empty desk.

Not a soul was there. The removal of her belongings made the sight look like a death. It just didn't look right. Zack exhaled as he pulled the desktop chair out and sunk down onto it. There was not a trace of her, he believed, until his fingers ran across a sticky note stuck beneath the letter tray poking its head out. He picked it out, smiling a little to himself as he recognised Claire's dainty handwriting. It was an old reminder to pick up bread on the way out of work, perhaps months old from its hidden presence.

God, what was he going to do?

Someone tapped his shoulder softly. Zack flinched a little before he swivelled the chair around. Jason was standing there, appearing a little apprehensive himself as he cleared his throat.

"Sorry, I didn't know—I guess." He paused, pushing his hands into his trouser pockets. "I guess I just didn't think Claire was like that," he finally said after what could have only seemed a desperate second or two to articulate the words.

Zack rejected his statement. "Claire didn't."

"I just assumed because of what Graves said this morning that—"

"Well, she didn't. Some bastard has had it out for her. And for you to think that Claire could actually do something like that is low—" He cut him off, narrowing his eyes as the shame shadowed over Jason's face.

"I *just*...Graves just went through it this morning, and when Claire didn't say anything the other day, I just *assumed*—I'm sorry. I feel like a bad friend. God, this isn't right," he admitted, bringing his hand to his forehead and rubbing back the short strands of blond hair in vexation.

Zack didn't say a word.

"Well...tell Claire hi from me, and if she needs a friend, I'm here," he finished, perhaps acknowledging Zack's silence as a sign for his presence to diminish.

Jason dispersed, and yet the silence of peace Zack hoped for was interrupted by the worst human Zack could think of. *Graves*. He stopped inside the cubicle, suspicious it seemed of Zack occupying the supposed desolate space. His blue shirt was creased around the collar, and his grey hair was bedraggled and looked like it needed a cut. Bags of sleep rested under his eyes, showing his war with sleep.

"I didn't expect anyone to be in here,"

Graves muttered rather quietly, his lips twitching and moving uncomfortably over one another. Perhaps he was going to investigate, search for any remaining clues that could give him insight to Claire's involvement. The cubicle was empty besides the computer, keyboard, tower, and mouse.

Zack lifted his left brow. He was intentionally prying as he asked Graves the simple question. "Do you really think Claire conspired against the company?"

"Mr. Chase, I believe the evidence. If that's what the board has found, then of course, I have no doubts, but to put my hundred percent confidence in what they've decided...I must admit it was a shame and a surprise to hear that my top employee was behind the motive. But that's just that," he replied, his underlining tone sinister.

Zack wanted more than anything to confront Graves right here and now, to expose the truth and watch the fear flicker in his eyes, but he chose against. He had to extract the vital information about the mysterious accomplice first before striking Graves off the list. *How was the question.*

"Now if you don't mind, Mr. Chase, I need to make the final checks to ensure there's nothing incriminating that Miss Winter has left behind. *You never know,*" he stated.

Zack stood up, trying his best to remain calm

as he exited the cubicle.

***

CLAIRE

What was one supposed to do with all this free time? Twiddle your thumbs? Sit by the apartment window staring out onto the street and counting the cars as they passed by? *Oh, look, that's three yellow cars I've seen go by! Or, oh look, I wonder what that person is up to!*

Her sanity was on its last thread. She couldn't stand this. She should be at work, not lounging at home. It's not like she had any choice until she managed to get another job. But at this point, she was completely losing motivation knowing her choices were very limited with consideration of her new, flashing record warning employers to stay away from her. *Who could trust someone who conspired against their company?* Even if you're innocent. *No one.*

Claire had thought about visiting Darren in person. She had yet to tell him of her news. She didn't blame him for not contacting her yesterday; he had a lot on his plate, which was why she decided against going to visit. He needed his space. Claire didn't want to add her own problem onto him. And besides, it seemed more than sensible and necessary to save her spare change that could have been used for the bus, for the possibility of remaining jobless at this point. *What if she had to get state welfare? What if no one would hire her?* Her nagging thoughts were desperate. Claire was sure she going to have a breakdown at this point.

The hours were dragging on by. Claire had achieved nothing. She'd probably switched sitting positions twice as she had flickered through the channels on the TV and must have gotten up three times to attend to her necessary needs of food and using the bathroom. But other than that, each second, minute, and hour felt like an eternity. An eternity in hell. She wanted Zack here. She wanted his company. At least the thought that he would return later was a comfort.

Claire was near enough falling asleep for the third time this morning until her attention was shaken by the series of gentle knocks upon the front door.

Her posture was sluggish and slow as she trailed over, not expecting much other than perhaps the postman needing a signature for a parcel. She opened the door, pleasantly surprised and thankful to see her mother standing there holding her arms at the ready. Claire pretty much raced into her arms, inhaling the sweet lavender scent of her mother's perfume dabbed on the cotton cloth of her purple jumper, and instantly melted into the bubble of protection reminding her of home and her juvenile existence.

"Mom, I-I didn't know y-you were coming," Claire began, a blubbering mess as she pulled back.

Claire's mother smiled warmly, entering across the threshold of the apartment and placing her brown leather handbag on the sideboard lined up against the wall.

"Honey, I would have come late last night. I just couldn't risk having your father sleeping at the steering wheel. He was up late messing on his bloody mechanics." She gently rolled her eyes. "He would have come with me now, but he's wrapped up in helping Matt for the wedding. He sends his love and is so sorry for your job," she explained, pulling off her loose blue jacket.

"It's fine, honestly. I'm just glad you've come," Claire replied, offering to hang her coat up onto the hooks where Claire's own and Zack's were hanging dormant.

"Oh, honey. I'm so sorry about all of this. I just don't understand how they've done this to you. We'll have to get someone official, a lawyer or something, to fight your case. It's just ridiculous that you've been dismissed," her mother went on, her facial expression sympathetic.

"There's no point, Mom. They've got some

pretty darn good evidence that makes me look completely guilty. I just feel like...my life's fucked now," Claire said miserably as she took to perch on the arm of the sofa.

Her mother followed suit, folding her arms as she gently sat on the sofa. "You'll get through this, Claire. You know me and your father will support you in any way. You always have a home back at home."

"I know, Mom. Thank you."

"God, your brother's getting married in the next two weeks and my daughter has been wrongly accused of this. It's not right. We're all supposed to be looking forward to Matt's wedding," she sighed.

"And we still will, Mom," Claire reassured as she clasped her mother's hand and squeezed it once. "I'm not going to let this ruin Matt's wedding. I'll find a job. Besides, Zack will help me out as much as I'll let him—"

"Oh, my! Yes! This Zack! Honey." She frantically clasped both Claire's hands. "The man you spoke about on the phone. Your roommate? And yes! Oh, Darren. Oh, honey. How is he doing? Oh, dear Claire. I'm so sorry I didn't come sooner, I—"

"Mom, Mom, don't worry," Claire interrupted, soothing her to calm down as she squeezed both her hands this time. "It's fine. It's not like you ignored my calls. So, it's all good. I'm just so glad you're here now. I feel like I'm going crazy being cooped up."

Claire's mother gently smiled. "So," she began, switching the subject. "This *Zack*—"

"We're together," Claire interjected, a sheepish smile accompanying her absolute truth. There was no point lying about that. She and Zack couldn't have been more official, so what was there to hide? She could tell even as those words left her lips, her mother was brewing with revelation and complete excitement.

"What! Oh Claire!" she said, flabbergasted. "You kept that a secret! *Oh, honey!* That's great news. Since when have you been dating? And why didn't you tell me sooner?"

"It's complicated, Mom," Claire replied truthfully. "I think we've also just got closer since…Darren lost…" Her words dissipated, knowing it was a difficult topic to bring up. It hadn't been a surprise that since that tragic night there was the odd flashes intruding into dreams late at night. It was another reason why she was so grateful for Zack; he was there, holding her in his arms when the nightmare would jump into her slumber. It seemed more frequent during those two weeks worrying over her job.

"Are you sure you don't need to see a therapist or something like I said on the phone?" she asked.

Claire shook her head. "I'll be fine. It's

impacted Darren more."

"Well." Her mother frowned a little. "Just promise me you will if it doesn't get better. Witnessing something like that is hard. You have to be lucky not to have it effect you in some way."

"I promise, Mom. Don't worry."

Her mother briefly scanned the apartment before suggesting, "Claire, I don't want you cooped up in here today. I think we should go out. I'm presuming you haven't gotten a dress for Matt's wedding, knowing how last minute you are, so I'll take you out. It will help take your mind off things."

"I just—"

"No isn't an answer. So, come on. And I want to hear more about this Zack, too."

CHAPTER FOUR

ZACK

What could he possibly do? What was next? His fingers ran across the rough stubble underneath his chin as he blankly stared at the swarm of people trailing in and out of the cafeteria. *What was all the point of this? Face it, Graves and whoever had won.* He should just give up.

He had no appetite as he kicked the cube of chicken with his fork.

"Hang on. You would like to meet?"

Zack's head rotated to the right as he heard Graves' voice swiftly intrude into his space. The man looked like he was on a mission. Maybe this was the opportunity.

Leaving his untouched chicken salad, Zack hastily sped after Graves, following him through the fire exit out onto the side of the

46

building.

They weren't completely alone. There was the odd smoker fulfilling the needs of nicotine leaning against the wall. Graves dashed past them, heading around the corner. Zack wasn't so far behind, cautiously keeping back in case he needed to flee from the scene.

"*Yes,* sorry. I just needed to get outside," he heard Graves reply. Zack got out his phone, pretending to appear interested in whatever was on the screen. "I—I, yes. I don't know what to say." Graves chuckled anxiously. "When?" "Friday? Okay. The—*what?*" A pause for a second or two. "The Lofts? Yeah, I know where that is. I can be there. Seven? Sure," Graves added, conveniently summarising the arrangements that were possible to leading him towards the puppeteer behind his own strings. *And if not,* it was one lousy date to unexpectedly arrive onto.

***

CLAIRE

Claire's mother had been cooing at several dresses she had pretty much forced her daughter to try on. The style was disgusting, and she was not going to pretend she was thrilled by her mother's choices. After searching through rack by rack, the ideal dress was found in the sales rack: a simple baby blue Bardot dress that was far cheaper than the £90 to £160 dresses her mother had chosen. After all, she was not a bridesmaid, she was on the groom's side, so she was thankful she could at least dictate her choice—although that didn't stop her mother, who in the end won when selecting the shoes.

"Mom," Claire groaned as her mother ushered her to walk down the aisle. "They fit, okay? I beg you to stop making me walk around like an idiot."

"Sweetie, let your mother at least feel like she isn't fifty-seven years old with a grown-up daughter. Besides, I know best, and by the looks of those heels, I'd say I chose the right pair. The ones you chose would have blistered the backs of your heels in the first hour of wearing them." Her mother plopped a pair of glasses into her brown leather handbag.

Claire rolled her eyes as she sat down onto the plush footstool and began taking off the heels. "Dear god."

"So, you haven't said a lot about this Zack," her mother said, hinting that she wanted a full chronological account of their relationship.

"Well, I haven't had the chance. I don't know…we're together? Is that enough?" Claire replied. Her mother's face flashed displeasure. "Okay, fine. I needed a roommate. I was falling short on my rent. The landlord had put it up, and he answered my ad. Long story cut short, but it just happened. I don't know what else you want me to say," she explained, slipping her feet back into her trainers.

"And does he treat you good?"

"Yes."

"Do you love him?"

"Y-yes…I do," Claire said almost in a whisper.

"Aw," her mother sighed gently. "I'm just happy that you've met someone, Claire. I honestly wouldn't have thought this day could have come," she teased with a snort.

"*Mom*! You make me out to be a nun sometimes," Claire chuckled.

***

Claire got back to her apartment around six. Her mother would have stayed, but she did have some trek to get home. Zack was sitting on the couch lazily flicking through some magazine when she headed in.

"Hey, how was your day?" he asked, throwing the magazine to the side as he jumped to his feet and headed for her.

"It was okay. I spent most of it with my mother. I'm glad she came over. It sucks being cooped up here all day now officially being jobless, let alone those two weeks I had to. How was yours?" she responded, accepting Zack's embrace.

"Eh, it was okay. Graves was being the usual dick. People just are," Zack said with a glint of humour.

"You're right on that," she agreed then lightly kissed his lips before pulling back from their embrace. "Ah, *fuck*," she sighed. "What am I seriously going to do, babe? I-I just have no idea what I'm supposed to do. Do *you* really think someone could have set me up? Or was it just an error in the—"

Zack followed her into the kitchen, where she popped on the kettle. "Honestly, I do. An error wouldn't have fucked up shit like this."

"But why? Why would someone do this?"

"Save their own back? Jealousy?" Zack suggested.

Claire shrugged her shoulders. "I don't even know anymore."

"Hey, I've booked us a reservation at The Lofts on Friday at seven. Meet me there?" Zack asked.

"Is this...*like a date*?" Claire coyly purred.

Zack grinned playfully. "Maybe...maybe not."

Claire tapped the end of his nose. "Well...Mr. Chase. I'd love to."

As she went to retract her fingers away, Zack grasped them gently and brought them to the edge of his lips. The admiration written in his eyes forced a bold blush upon her cheeks.

"Did I ever tell you how beautiful you are?" he softly said before kissing her fingertips.

Claire melted. "Not enough times," she teased.

There was that playful grin bouncing onto the scene. "I mean it. You are so beautiful, Claire. I love your smile," he replied, now gently massaging his right fingers behind the back of her earlobe.

"Are you trying to seduce me, Mr. Chase?"

"That's the plan. Can I get admission to…your bed?" His voice husky and dangerous as the flicker of desire took over his face.

"I…suppose I could agree to that," Claire flirted.

It didn't take much convincing as their lips met in unison. It was fervent passion that drove Claire to insanely to drive her begging lips against his. His hands slid around her waist as the thirst of their tongues vehemently attacked in a teasing slide over the other. Claire gasped at the growl at the back of his throat.

Zack led Claire towards the kitchen counter, her back making contact against it as he kissed her neck, teasing behind her ear whilst she tried her hardest to remain still. It felt like ecstasy; she wanted nothing more than to feel him close. Claire began aggressively attacking his collar, undoing the buttons as his lips remained to suck and kiss the side of her neck. Soon enough, he was shirtless, hungry, and tearing away at her t-shirt and jeans combined.

"*Zack.*" She gasped, feeling the fervid flicker of his tongue upon her breasts. He hadn't even unhooked the bra and she was turned on. Her back naturally arched forward as her fingers raked through his hair, watching as he continued to trail a line of kisses down the centre of her torso, stopping just before the edge of her black knickers.

"I need you now," she said breathlessly, observing how his lips curled in agreement. In a blink, she had her legs wrapped around his torso as he carried her out of the kitchen towards her bedroom. They shared their episodes of breathless laughs as they headed down the corridor, nearly falling into the wall a couple times from the hunger of their ravaging lips.

Zack gently dropped her on the bed, climbing on top of her before his lips dived in deep, kissing her.

Zack unhooked her bra, throwing it on the floor. Claire was half exposed, and she enjoyed feeling his greedy lips nipping and sucking her hardened nipples. Claire wanted this. He wanted this.

"Look at…you," Zack muttered in between kissing her breasts. "Goddamn, Claire…you're just so *beautiful*."

She couldn't help but blush, even if it only lasted for a second before the overwhelming organic lust filled her system. Her hands helplessly went for his buckle. A dark growl echoed from the back of his throat as he complied, undoing them, and all too soon, he was completely naked.

Zack smirked, shaking his head down at her before his hands suddenly tore her knickers in half, *literally*. Claire gasped feeling his member throbbing at the point of entrance.

And then before Claire anticipated it, she felt him enter her. It was beyond passion stirring between them as Claire clawed her nails into his back, begging in his ear. Their bodies rocked together, their breathless voices drained from the exhilarating feel of their spirts connecting *intimately*. His hip bones moved gently against her then harder, making her walls inside throb at the build up inside of her.

"Fuck," she could hear him grunt, quickening the pace.

And then it happened. Claire released soon after he did, her body consequently high on cloud nine. She was breathless and so was he. But it didn't stop Claire nor him from wanting more, so when Claire took a turn to climb on top of him, she was high on the addiction of him.

Chapter Five

ZACK

It was another spontaneous get together at the Bensons' household...the usual order of his cold, stubborn mule of a father eating in silence whilst suspiciously eyeing those sitting around the table, his mother squabbling on like a turkey and Jared just as fed-up as Zack, wishing they were elsewhere than here.

At least Zack could look forward to tomorrow. Graves' dinner date could be the jackpot to finding out who was manipulating him behind the scenes.

"Not long now, Zack," his father announced, startling the room. Members of the kitchen staff scuttled quickly out the room, leaving the family alone in private. Whenever Elijah had something to say, it was usually important, and any who did not share the last name of Benson was expected to vanish quicker than lightning.

"What?" Zack said, jabbing his fork into the piece of salmon.

"Your revival," his father snorted, finding amusement as he dabbed the corner of his lips with the white cloth napkin.

Zack rolled his eyes in annoyance. "Funny."

"*Zack,* less of that attitude. You're not to disrespect your father like that," his mother interjected, frown lines creasing across her forehead.

"It's okay, love. Our son just needs to learn some manners," Elijah said contemptuously. There was an uncomfortable pause. Jared shuffled in his chair, looking quickly at his lap as the tension between Zack and their father thickened.

Zack bit down on his tongue, refusing to let his old man bark him into confrontation.

"So are you prepared? I shouldn't expect any funny ideas or anything, should I?" Elijah asked, his left brow propped up in suspicion.

"No, I'm prepared," Zack lied, knowing fully aware that he had been working on reviving whatever had been lost because of Graves and whoever had been interfering. *Was that a thing he wanted to mention to his father? That someone was working on the inside?* Zack had thought over it but refused to allow his father to brag in vain over Zack's failure to uphold security.

"Good. It will be nice to finally have you on the same side for once, Zack," he said, toasting his wine glass into the air.

***

Friday had come around the corner. It had been three days since Claire lost her job, two weeks since her whole suspension at work, and more than enough time spent dwelling on the fact that eventually Zack would have to tell the truth once everything came out.

He was anxious, felt sick to his stomach all day. He had kept a cautious eye on Graves, watching his every move whilst reassuring himself that tonight wouldn't be a waste. It had to have something to do with Graves' behind the scenes deal with whoever was pulling his strings. If it happened to be some other arrangement that conveniently seemed suspicious, then Zack knew there would be very little he could do after that.

Last night's uncomfortable meal with his father had shaken him to want to succeed. He wanted to smoke out the traitorous pair, Graves and whoever. He wanted to prove to his father that sustainability was profitable, and finally, then be seen and take full control of what was his father's domain. It seemed do-able. Everything was just relying on *tonight*.

By five-thirty, Zack had returned home to the apartment, disheartened to see Claire sighing into her coffee mug, unaware of his presence until he gave a short cough.

Immediately, she sat up and, from what he could see, sprung into that "I'm seriously okay" mood when Zack knew that wasn't the entire truth. He could imagine how miserable she felt, lounging around here all day feeling hopeless.

"Hey," she greeted, smiling as she got up from her chair and headed over to him. She pecked his cheek and fell into his embrace. "How was your day?"

"All right. Nothing…interesting," Zack replied, feeling the usual guilt of bile rise up his throat. "Any…luck?"

Claire moved back, collecting her mug as she took it over to the sink. "Nope. Even a supermarket won't take me. They asked for a reference to my last workplace, and of course, it would be printed in red and black, the big warning about this employee." She jerked her thumb at her chest and rolled her eyes.

"Ah, I'm sorry—"

"Let's just…could we not talk about it? I just want to have a good night tonight. Just me and you. I just want to forget this week," she interjected, squeezing his bicep gently as she passed him and went to exit the kitchen. "I'm gonna start getting changed," she added, leaving him alone in the room.

Zack was stuck between helplessly admiring Claire from across the table and keeping an eye out for Graves to lead him hopefully to the traitor. She looked as beautiful as ever. Her brown locks floated across her bare shoulders, the body-hugging black sleek dress accentuated her curves, and that wonderful smile lit up the whole room.

"Zack, thank you for this," she said, pushing a strand of hair behind her ear bashfully. "I'm just so glad that…well, that I have you." Her cheeks reddened.

"Babe." Zack slid his hand across the table to grasp hers. "I'm glad that I have you. Honestly, I don't know what I would do without you sometimes." And he meant that. He had to be thankful for that lousy bet; it gave him something worth more than his money. He could only hope that once the truth came to surface, things between them could remain the same. But deep down, he knew a relationship built on lies and deceit could only crumble.

Claire snorted. "That's even cheesy for you."

Zack chuckled. "I know. What have you done to me, Claire?"

It was nearing seven. Zack had remained attentive to his wristwatch, Claire, and the front entrance, wondering when that leech of a man would arrive.

"So, are you looking forward to attending my brother's wedding as my date?" Claire asked, placing her flute of champagne down after taking a sip or two of the bubbly alcoholic drink.

"*Date?* Hm. I just thought we were friends," he teased. "Okay…friends who are very intimate then."

Claire rolled her eyes playfully. "Yeah, well. I just can't believe my brother is getting married. I mean…if you ever knew my brother when we were kids, he was always on about how he would never marry and he would live like Tarzan or something, going on mad adventures. And now…" She let out a huge breath of air. "He's actually settling down."

"Hm, well, he's trapping himself."

"Oi." Claire gently smacked his hand, finding amusement in his cheeky comment.

They shared laughter in the situation.

"But…have you ever thought about marriage?" Claire innocently asked.

Zack nearly choked on the mouthful of prawns he'd just consumed. "W—wow. Way to make a man nearly choke to death," he teased as he slapped his chest.

"Seriously, though. Have you?"

Zack dabbed around his lips with the white cloth. "I…haven't, if I'm honest." He looked down at his lap, afraid to see Claire's reaction, but once he dared to look up, she didn't appear offended or put off. Instead, a sense of intrigue fell upon her face. "I—*never* really thought of myself and marriage. I mean commitment…was a lot for me."

"*Interesting*." Claire coyly smiled.

"What?" An amused smile targeted his own.

"Nothing…anyway, tell me something funny," she replied.

It was difficult to not become absorbed by that infectious laugh of hers; it had nearly cost him missing Graves arriving through the front door. Zack had to excuse himself, saying he was going to pop to the gentlemen's and then order drinks from bar, with the real intention of following the man in the blue mismatched suit.

Graves was being escorted by a waiter, who led him through the main room and out of sight. Zack was aware of the more private space for those more privileged wishing absolute isolation from the ordinary folk in the main dining hall.

How was he supposed to get in? He needed to know. He needed to get in. Zack was leaning his right elbow on the bar counter after ordering two lemon and Archers for himself and Claire. He gave a quick glance to Claire. Thank god her back was facing him.

In the archway, a bouncer stood in sight with the traffic of the waiting staff entering and exiting the private space where the wealthy and those seeking extra attention sat. *Perhaps money could persuade? Or a wardrobe change?* He had to do something if he wanted to pry into Graves' business.

And then out of nowhere, an opportunity arose. One of the waiting staff, hot and sweaty, slid off their jacket, conveniently placing it on the chair underneath the front desk. They stood there for a second or two dabbing their forehead with a handkerchief before returning to the traffic of staff entering and leaving the kitchen.

Now was his time. Zack left a note on the side, asking if his drinks could be kept aside whilst he excused himself very quickly, and then snaked through the hall towards the desk. In between that quick walk, he looked back and forth for any apparent threats and whether Claire was where she still was. *She hadn't moved, good.*

Pretending to grab some menus, Zack grasped the jacket and quickly scooted towards the bathroom with large strides. Once inside, he slid the jacket on, thankful for the pinned name tag on the blazer pocket. He only hoped the bouncer wasn't on a friendly level with this particular staff member.

Zack left the bathroom, passed and grabbed the menus he had messily discarded on the desk, and then headed for the private space. His heart was hammering, pounding like drums over and over.

Trying to appear confident, he refrained from eye contact as he took two strides forward. The bouncer gave him a quick look-over before returning in his composed state. *He was in.* Zack sighed gently, dropping the menus on another desk that held extra cutlery and a desktop lit up with the layout of the restaurant, and then went on his mission to find Graves.

There were several round booths, isolated by long red curtains hiding each inhabitant inside.

He couldn't just open them and peek in. That would just decapitate his cover. Instead, Zack remained attentive, listening as he passed each booth and dodged the odd employee making their returns to attend to their guests.

"Gerald, I really thought you would have been pleased—" He heard a dainty, high-pitched voice as Zack stood by the first booth hidden beneath the robe of curtains.

"Honey, I really don't care if you have an affair with the pool boy or become a swinger as long as you don't get caught. Do whatever you please. You know how this marriage works," another deeper voice returned with.

Trouble in paradise, Zack speculated as he pulled back and continued on towards the next booth.

It wasn't the second booth, either. It was another troublesome couple moaning, and the third booth gave Zack no hope.

Until then with luck, the fourth booth became the jackpot. Any idiot could recognize that snake's voice. Zack stood close by, cautiously keeping an eye out for any signs of the staff catching on to his suspicious behaviour whilst attentively listening to what he could make out that was happening in the booth.

"So, is this it? Or—" That was Graves speaking. He sounded pathetic.

"For now, *yes.*"

Another male's voice. *Was this the perpetrator?* Zack had to lean in more. Something seemed so familiar about that voice.

"I think we've made it pretty clear, and it should send a message. I still expect you to contact me if any new changes occur and anything you believe will threaten the company's foundation," the male spoke, sounding self-assured and rather intimidating.

Zack froze. *Why did they sound so familiar?* He didn't want to believe it, but in the pit of his stomach, it sounded like his father. *Could he believe his father would have stooped this low to jeopardize his son?* It couldn't be. *But what if it was?*

"As for those emails, don't be as sloppy next time. You cost yourself a valuable employee," they added, a hidden spit of warning in the back of their throat.

"Yes, I promise that won't happen again. I do apologise sincerely, Mr. Benson," Graves replied anxiously.

Zack swallowed. *Fuck.*

"I suppose it shocks you."

"Yes, I—I hadn't expected the old CEO—"

"Well, just keep it to yourself. Now, shall we celebrate with the lobster, Graves?"

And there it was. The information Zack needed. It suddenly felt hotter in the room. Zack undid his collar button, slid the waiter's jacket off, and threw it onto the floor as he escaped from the area.

As he left the room, Zack felt the urge to punch something. *Preferably his father.* Zack knew how about his father despised his ideas, but to stoop that low? It was ridiculous. It should have been something he expected. Why he hadn't put two and two together?

***

CLAIRE

She had surveyed the room about twice, maybe four times, hoping to spot Zack. He'd been gone quite a while, which made her twitchier and more concerned that something bad had happened. *Had he slipped in the bathroom? Got into a fight outside with some rude, drunk guest? Or had he slipped out, not wanting or meaning anything he said to her?*

Then out of nowhere, she spotted him carrying two short glasses, heading for their table.

"Where have you been?" she asked, curious

to the red flush that was refusing to leave his face.

"Sorry—I was—getting drinks," he said, placing them down before hastily getting into his seat.

"Is everything all right? You seem pissed off. Did something happen?" Claire inquired, confident from his uptight posture and heavy sips from the glass that he was angered by something or someone.

"No—*yeah,* I'm fine," he replied.

For the rest of that evening, Claire knew but wasn't sure how far she could pry as Zack remained a little distant and annoyed.

CHAPTER SIX

A full week had passed. Claire had not received any good news from the jobs she had applied for, and Zack had the trouble of biting his lip as he worked harder throughout the entire week, trying to devise a plan that could bypass his father, the man who was behind both Claire's fall and his own. *His attack had to be unexpected. Like father, like son.*

How on earth one could do that to their own son? wondered Zack. But this was Elijah Benson. It shouldn't have come as a surprise.

And now with the magazine just literally days away, there was the impending threat of Claire finding out the truth. Something he was starting to think he should have told her earlier about with their new-found relationship.

***

CLAIRE

"Now, are you sure we have everything?" Claire asked again, causing Zack to sigh in frustration.

"Yes, *babe.* We have everything. What more could we need? You've packed our toothbrushes, which I didn't pack earlier. So I think we're okay."

Claire scanned the bedroom once more than necessary then briefly glanced towards the suitcase at the foot of the bed. "I just don't want to forget anything because I always tend to. Now, did I pack—"

"Do you need your sanitary towels or tampons?" Zack interrupted, casually asking her as he flopped onto the bed and rested his head behind his propped-up arms.

"No." She shook her head, still looking around her room. "I'm not on till next week. And could you please be a little more helpful than just lying back like you're on your holiday?" she scolded as she scurried around the bed and headed for her bedside table.

"Lighten up," Zack said, smiling before he sat up. He tugged her arm and pulled her back against him on the bed. "Now, just relax." Claire snorted and fidgeted a little at the ticklish sensation of his words below her earlobe.

"Zaaaack," she groaned, trying to get up but failing miserably as he continued to tighten the embrace securing her petite body frame. "I—need—to get—up, ow, ow. My hair—get up, you fat pig!" She whacked and kicked her legs about as he rolled on top of her, suffocating her ribcage.

"Say please," he teased, rolling the tip of his nose against her cheeks. "Say please."

"Fuck you!" She huffed, trying with all her strength to push him off. "You're gonna squash me! Zack!" Still he failed to move, and she was alarmed by the sudden arousal she felt by his digging member against her. "Okay, please! Please!" she begged, a little relieved yet at the same time disappointed his companion took a walk about, too.

"You know," he said, sitting up and caressing his fingers against her heated cheeks, "I love it when you squeal."

Claire rolled her eyes as she sat up, messy strands of hair sticking to the sides of her forehead. "Too bad you can't do that in bed," she teased with a wink.

"You cheeky son of a bitch," Zack hissed playfully before grasping her head and bringing her lips against his with wolfish need. Her hands ran through his hair as he pushed her back in the soft heaven of the quilt, his tongue skimming the surface of the inside of her mouth and his hands constantly squeezing the life out of her ass like kneading bread. "I love you." He stopped for air. Claire smiled, her cheeks burning alight.

"I love you," she replied, wrapping her arms around his neck. "Now, why did you stop?"

Another half an hour or so and they could at last say they were ready to hit the road. A taxi driver called Barry turned up outside the apartment to drive them. Juggling the one suitcase into the boot of the car, Zack soon joined Claire in the back of the car where she was having a small natter with the man who looked as if he should be rallying in a boxing match. Fierce biceps, bushy greyish moustache, and golden hoop earrings running all up the side of each ear. Yet when he heard the fella speak, it appeared he had a soft touch. "So, lovely day isn't it? Going somewhere nice this weekend?"

"Yeah, something like that," Claire replied as she searched through her purse. "Sorry," she apologised to the driver, looking towards him at the rear mirror. "I get a little paranoid when making sure I've got everything. Yeah, me and my boyfriend here are going to my brother's wedding." She was given full interest from the driver ahead, who nodded and smiled like he was a cooing mother at a child's school play.

"That's sounds lovely. Me and the wife are taking our caravan down this weekend to go fishing and whatnot. Gotta make the most of this weather, don't we?" He suddenly came out with a pair of sunglasses and propped them on.

"We do," Claire agreed. "So, erm. Yeah,

we're heading to Worcestershire. I've got the address here." She struggled to undo her seatbelt at first as she handed over a piece of paper and instructed the driver with a few more added details. Whilst this was occurring, her phone began to ring, so being the gentleman Zack was, he answered. "Hello. Claire can't talk at the moment. Who is this?"

"Oh, hi, it's Darren," the raspy, fragile voice of the broken-hearted man said. "I can call back later. I—"

"Oh, no. She won't be long. How—how you are doing, Darren?" Zack asked awkwardly.

"I'm…okay, thank you for asking," Darren replied after a brief pause of silence. "I'm just okay."

At this point, Claire sat back and looked over after sorting out the journey with the driver and realised that Zack was talking with someone on her phone. With a final word of consolation, Zack passed the phone over, leaving Claire to privately listen to what her friend had to say. Darren talked to her for the majority of the ride. Eventually, she pulled the phone back from her ear.

"Sorry." She looked over to Zack. "He was telling me about…some dreams he's had lately."

"No, that's fine. What dreams?" Zack asked.

Claire exhaled as she rested back in the seat. "He sees Jonas in his dreams. Like he believes he's trying to tell him something. I honestly don't know, but I just hate him feeling like this. I know it's out of grief, but what if the Jonas in his dreams…is, you know? Telling him things like—"

"Don't think like that," Zack blurted out and grasped her hand. "Don't you think like that, baby."

Claire nodded then inhaled. "You're right."

"So, *your* parents?"

"What about my parents?"

Zack rubbed his jawline with his other free hand as he muttered, "They're not eccentric, right? Not hippies or anything? You know those naked-ass people who—"

"Oh, god no!" Claire howled out with laughter. "I mean…my mother can be a handful at times, but they're great people. Aw, baby," she cooed, squeezing his cheek. "You'll be adorable. So, don't go whimpering. Put your big boy nappy on."

Zack smirked, playfully shoving her hand away as he looked towards his lap. "You can be an arsehole sometimes."

"I know, but that's why you love me."

The driver upfront suddenly cursed aloud as he slowed down the car. "Do pardon my language. We've hit traffic," he said, pointing his hand out ahead where a sea of cars, lorries, and the odd motorcyclist stood in barely shifting congestion.

"Well, that's gonna tick off my mother," Claire sighed as she smiled briefly over towards Zack. "Well, then handsome. *Entertain* me."

CHAPTER SEVEN

CLAIRE

"God, that was the most awful, long, and tiring journey in history. And the taxi driver? Yeah, lovely he was, but he never shut up. I was tempted to get out the car, usher him out, and drive myself," Claire groaned as she rested the back of her hand against her forehead. Zack smirked as he tugged on the suitcase's handle as they began heading down the gravel driveway, the sound of crunching consistently following after and ahead. "And you just sat there, mister! Leaving poor little ol' me to talk to the man. Like, god, how many—"

"Claire!" A shrill voice echoed through Claire's eardrums. "Oh, you're here, my darling. Late, but here." The familiar tone of scolding could only belong to her mother, the woman whose complaints to the store's manager could authorise them to a year's supply of teabags. She was really that good. Even before Claire could breathe a single word, she was suffocated in a tight embrace.

"Okay, Mom," Claire said through gritted teeth. "You can let go of me now."

It wasn't that simple with her mother latching on for a further ten seconds before she elegantly retracted and her eyes sauntered over towards the gentleman standing behind their little reunion. Then she spoke in a poised manner, "And *who* is this?"

Claire rolled her eyes at her mother's pretentious display, rearing up to introduce Zack when the sudden outburst of her mother racing up to Zack and engulfing him into a hug startled her.

"I know who this is!" Claire's mother yelped as she clawed her nails into his back. She sure was a hugger. "This is the handsome fella you've been on about. Oh my, I'm Linda." She blushed as she pulled back and deliberately curled a finger around his jaw. "He is a fine fella. How old are you—"

"*Mom*," Claire hissed as she grabbed her mother's hand with a golden wedding ring around her fourth finger.

"Oh, Claire. I tease," her mother said, rolling her eyes. "Now, let's go inside." She gestured with her hands like an eager zookeeper trying to persuade the animal to follow. Zack headed in first, shrugging his shoulders as he smirked, leaving the astounded Claire to sigh at her mother's display.

"So, tell me, Zack, what do you like about my daughter?" her mother asked. *God*, she cringed. So, whilst leaving Zack to the vexation that could be her mother sometimes, she headed into the second room on the right where she knew her father would be either snoring his head off or tinkering around with some car parts that her mother strongly protested being in the house.

"*Dad.*" Claire smiled as she entered the room, finding correctly that her father, Andy, was fiddling with some part that belonged to a car's exhaust. "Trust you to find you here doing this. Where's Matty? Or when is he coming around?" she inquired as she slid onto the sofa beside him.

"Well, I think he's still recovering from his hangover yesterday. The lads had him tied to a streetlamp, and he was pissed. Also," Andy said, pausing as he ushered Claire to come closer as he whispered, "I don't think either of us wants to be coming home when you know your mother can give you ten times the smothering and headache."

Claire giggled at her father's tease, feeling as always like that small, special girl. "Dad, he's here," Claire said, trying to restrain herself from squealing.

"Who?"

Claire hugged one of the pillows as she replied with excitement, "Zack. My boyfriend, you know?"

Andy gasped playfully, holding his free hand clasped over his mouth. "You brought a boy home, Claire? Oh *no, no, no*. We can't be having that, can we?" He tutted with pretence. "And where is this boy? In your bed? Did you sneak him in last night?"

Claire nodded, playing along. "Oh, yes! And he climbed up into the window!" Gasping, she broke out of character as she chuckled at her father holding his hands against his cheeks in disgrace and evading his eyes from her own.

"I'm so disappointed, Claire. And where is this vile boy now?"

"Mom," Claire sneered.

"Ouch."

Just then, her mother and Zack appeared, entering the room as lively as ever. "Andy, put that away, will you?" Frowning, she flicked her finger towards her husband. "We have a guest. Or rather…Claire's boyfriend."

"Hello, you must be the boy she snuck into her room last night. Correct, Claire?" her father teased, ignoring his wife's imperative to put away the car part he continued to clean with a rag.

"Oh, yes, Dad. That's him, all right," Claire replied, her eyes solely locked onto Zack's with a radiant, cheeky grin expressed on her lips. His lips reflected back like a mirror image, confirming he was very well aware of what was going on. "What will you ever do to him?" She held her hand against her forehead to play as if she were a flustered damsel in distress.

"Hung, drawn, and quartered, of course," her father said before he placed the part on the side and stood up then shifted back into normal mode as he introduced himself to Zack. "All right, I'm Andy. I'd shake your hand, but I'm afraid it would make yours dirty. Zack, is it?"

"Yes, Zack is the name."

Andy smiled genuinely as he stated before passing by, "Well, any boyfriend of Claire's is a boyfriend of mine. I'm just gonna wash my hands."

"Andy, clean your mess up after you," her mother barked after as she hurriedly followed him into the kitchen.

Claire shook her head with amusement as she slapped the area next to her. "Come and sit your ass down, *Romeo*."

Zack slid down comfortably beside her, hugging his arm around her shoulders and pecking her cheek. "I like your folks," he said. "They're…casual. Not so uptight."

"Indeed, they are. How about my mom? What did she want? Was she pestering you?" Claire asked, intrigued to know any good things her mother may have said about her, if the past was mentioned, but more importantly what the man sitting beside her had said. Zack shrugged his shoulders deliberately, knowing he'd gain a response.

"Oi." Claire nudged him in the side of the torso with her elbow. "Tell me. Otherwise, you aren't sleeping in my old bed with me tonight."

Zack smirked. "I bet it's real squeaky, too, isn't it?"

"Fuck off, Zack."

Zack surrendered as he licked his bottom lip. "It was nothing much. Just your common meeting-the-parents type of questions. Not that I would really know, considering this is a first."

"Really?"

"Yes, *really*," Zack said earnestly. "I've never really met a girl's parents, and if I have, they wouldn't have known it was me messing about with their daughter. I swear to you, this is a first."

Claire's eyes lit up with humour. "Well done, Zack. You lost your I met-your-parents-virginity."

"Fuck you." He laughed as he snuggled her closer into his embrace and kissed the top of her forehead. She squirmed as she felt his hot breath tease across the skin. He licked her cheekbone. "Ass." She squealed as she tried to detangle herself.

"Hey?"

They stopped, and like lightning on a rod,

Claire stood up and raced into another's man arms. "Matty," she said, full of affection. "You're *here*."

"I'm here, and you?" He stopped as they pulled back from embrace. "How are you doing? That—"

"Don't worry. We can talk about that some other time. This is *your* weekend, not mine. You're getting fucking married!" she blurted out and then ruffled her brother's hair with the struggle to attempt to reach his staggering height.

"Oi, oi," he joked. "Not the hair. She'll kill me if a single strand is out of place."

"*Ugh*. Oh! And Matt, meet my…boyfriend." She timidly looked back over towards Zack, who casually waved. *"Zack."*

"Hey, nice to meet you. Although I'd be careful with this one; she's bats crazy." Matt snickered, returning the friendly wave.

"Hey," Claire gasped as she shoved her brother's shoulder. "He already knows that. Now go find the parents. Mom will kill you if you don't show your face. Go." She pointed her finger out the door and received a cheesy salute from Matt, who then staggered back into the hallway.

***

You know what Claire loved about weddings? Nothing. Suppose the food buffet was all right or the three-course meal give or take, but she was always put off by the ceremony. Funny considering she was the one who loved to curl in a ball and read for hours on end about starry-eyed, passionate plots where the rich boy, the high school jock, or the shy, unpopular nerd would get the girl. Perhaps those were the reasons why she was put off from weddings or it could be the fact the three-phrase saying was recycled to the point it had become meaningless. She wasn't against it, but she wouldn't jump straight into bed with the next man who popped down on one knee. No, just give her a committed partner and she'd be quite content. As for today, it didn't matter what she thought because her older, charming, and equally hideous brother was getting married to the love of his life.

"You know you look stunning," Zack uttered behind her, his grinning smile broadening as he ran his hands up and down either side of her arms, spawning goose bumps along the trail. Claire blushed a little as she felt his frame cuddle like a missing piece of the puzzle into the mould of her body; the reflection in the mirror projected their recognised lust.

"I like your ass in *that* suit," Claire chirped as she played with their entwined fingers. "Totally accentuates what you've already got, babe. I'd kill to get a squeeze of that."

"Speak for yourself," he countered before his hands greedily pinched her plump, round bum. "Feels to me there is an ass-planation needed." He chortled as Claire swiped his hands away with glee at his intended terrible pun.

"Come on, you," she nagged, pulling on his loose right hand. "We better get downstairs before I have my mother banging on the door and before I allow you to unzip this dress and we get back in *that* bed."

"Aye, aye, Captain," Zack joked with a salute and a swift slap on her ass. "I'll follow your orders."

Downstairs, the groom and the star of the afternoon and evening were being peppered with kisses by the one and only Mrs. Winter, who cradled Matt's face in the palms of her hands. Andy eventually had to step in, tackling his wife's fingers off the frame of his cheeks and gently led her back into place beside him.

"Come on, darling. He's doesn't want to be explaining himself for the mysterious appearance of red lipstick on his face," he teased, the usual humourous side the family was used to.

Mrs. Winter's bottom lip trembled for a few seconds before she turned and wailed with excitement at the emergence of Claire and Zack heading down the stairs. "Oh, you look beautiful! And you!" She shifted her attention towards Zack. "You handsome devil, you!" She was possibly near to fainting in Zack's arms if it weren't for Claire engaging in the commotion and ushering her quietly back towards their father's side.

Matt began to head for the door, lifting the latch when Mrs. Winter proclaimed, "Wait! We need photos. All of us together. Especially Claire and Zack together."

"Mom," Claire groaned. "We have a professional photographer who will take plenty throughout the day. Let's just go."

She dragged Zack along until her mother announced aloud again, "No, no. Just a picture of you two then. I just need a photo, darling. Andy, go get the camera off the side and you two stand there at the bottom of the stairs." Obliging, Claire and Zack headed into place, Claire whining a little before she composed herself and stood in position. Ideally, she would rather have the eyes of a stranger snapping photos than the sound of her mother cooing in the background as she rested her left hand against Zack's chest and smiled dead ahead. Nor did it help with Zack's hand caressing her hip, making her very aware that he knew where the lace of her knickers started and where they ended.

"Okay, okay, we can go!" Mrs. Winter spurred on, directing the entire family out of the household and straight on towards the classic car that Mr. Winter had done up especially for Matt's big day. The vivid blue car was decorated with banners announcing that it was their son's big day.

It was planned that Matt would head on along with their mother and their father would take Claire and Zack in their mother's car. Ahead, the engine of an old Austin Mini howled to life, engaging Zack's interest. He sat eagerly forward in the middle of the backseat to get a proper look.

"Like what you see?" Andy asked, noticing his daughter's boyfriend's engrossment.

"Very," Zack nodded. "How much work have you done on that?"

Claire could only roll her eyes as she detached herself from the conversation and focused on the passing scenery as both cars headed to the venue where the ceremony would take place. From what she was told, the venue was chosen by Mrs. Winter rather than Matt's soon-to-be-wife. It was located in the rural parts of Worcestershire, a country hall with idyllic views from outside, allowing guests to hop around the freshly mown lawn and stand under the blossoming cherry trees for a lovely photo or two. The ceremony and reception would all take place under one roof. It sounded nice, and when they arrived, the typical country hall was accentuated by the green, spiralling ivy crawling up against the walls and a large banner commending the couple's marriage. The weather also complimented nicely, blue skies and fairly still summer temperatures considering the year was progressing into autumn.

Matt was intercepted by gathering guests once they were in the hall, which began to fill up. It was there that Claire was greeted with other family, her grandparents and uncles and aunts, who all had the delight of meeting Zack. She was filled with pride to know this was the man who had taken her heart.

Soon the event was in full swing; guests were seated, hushed a little as they blabbered with excitement over the arrival of the bride. Up ahead, Claire's brother looked anxious, rubbing his palms together as he exhaled, knowing that any second she would be walking around that corner. It was such a proud moment for Claire, knowing that her older sibling was making the biggest commitment in his life. Good god, looking at him now made her realise just how time had changed, from his adorable, small dinosaur pyjamas he used to wear, to his black tuxedo with the polished leather Oxford shoes; no more Power Rangers slippers. Was she going to cry? Perhaps.

Then that well-known piece began. Guests stood up and smiles radiated as the blushing bride headed down the aisle beside her father. And indeed, she was beautiful. Claire wanted to cry seeing that admiration upon her brother's face as his fiancée made her final step to his side.

The marriage vows continued, as did Claire's strain of holding onto Zack's arm as she tried not to whimper and mimic the same emotion the ceremony was evoking upon her mother. But dear me, she thought, it was so beguiling to witness.

And just like that, the commitment was sealed. Not rocket science.

"Congratulations," Claire said, hugging her brother then her sister-in-law. "I'm so happy for you both." They thanked her before they were engulfed by yet another wave of people congratulating their marriage.

Zack held Claire close as they headed outside, where several guests were having their photos taken with the picturesque scenery.

"So, your brother is a married man," Zack declared as they sat on a bench underneath a cherry tree. "No getting out of that one now." He cuddled Claire as she rested her head on his shoulder.

"Yes." She giggled, looking down towards her open-toe heels and appreciating the dash of black nail paint across each toenail. "God, my brother is actually married. *Fuck me*." Lifting her head up, she shook her head with glee.

Zack laughed. "You make it seem as if he never was going to be."

"Well, he wasn't going to—although that was a pact he made when he was a kid, so—"

"So, yeah," Zack interjected as he shook his head, smiling. "I think that wasn't to be taken seriously, Miss Winter."

"Claire! Zack! Over here!" They turned their heads to see Claire's mother bellowing on the patio, ushering them to come over. "We're having photos taken, pronto!"

Two hours later after a mad session of photography and the digestion of food, the after-party was in full swing with a few dads on the floor embarrassing their teenagers with their awful dance moves. Some older women kicked off their heels as they hooted to the classics being played by the DJ. Claire's brother and sister-in-law were greeting and briefly discussing with guests the progression of the night. As for Claire, she had her feet kicked up on vacant chair, her head resting against Zack's shoulder as she quietly giggled from their intimate conversation. The flickering of the white candle reflected fiery orange shades upon their cheeks with the wax melting further down into the dish.

"You're such a dick," Claire chuckled as Zack nibbled her earlobe, enticing a ticklish sensation across her skin. "Such a—"

"Are you two not dancing?" Her mother's interruption halted their show of affection.

Claire shook her head, dazed a little as she

pulled Zack's arm across her body with a grin. "We're fine, Mom."

"Well, actually," Mrs. Winter paused, flicking her locks to the side of her shoulder, "I'd like your young man to take me around the dance floor then. Zack?" Her look was similar to when she would give Claire the I-know-so when Claire was asked what she had done wrong. It was both patronising and highlighted a flicker of amusement.

"Sure," Zack replied, lifting himself up as Claire sat up.

"You better bring him back, Mom," Claire teased before she received a quick peck on the cheek by Zack. Her mother laughed as she pretended to swoon. "Oh, I'll be a good girl, darling." Claire playfully rolled her eyes.

Claire sat back, pressing her lips subconsciously together as she tried to suppress the broadening smile as she watched Zack helplessly carry the lead of the dance; it was not debatable. Her mother was a bad dancer. Her father joined her, taking Zack's vacant seat.

"Hey kiddo," he said, slapping his knee and briefly sipping from his bottle of beer. "That's not your mother, is it? With your fella?"

"Yes, Dad," Claire replied, cringing as her mother circled the wrong way on the dance floor. "God." She laughed along with her father. "Mom really can't dance. Should we tell her that?"

"Honey, that was one secret I kept from your mother for thirty years." He chuckled, shaking his head. "But it's one thing I'll never change about her." His confession of endearment touched Claire's heart.

Eventually they returned, Claire's mother breathlessly blabbering on. "Oh, I'm a dancer all right. I was wonderful, wasn't I?" Zack smiled. He exhaled with exhaustion as he flopped onto the chair located on the other side of Claire and reached for his drink.

"Honey, you were spectacular. Always are, my *dear*." Mr. Winter cheered, grasping her hand and squeezing it with affection. Mrs. Winter blushed. "Oh, Andy. You should—oh my God!" she suddenly yelped as the announcement of the bride and groom's dance in the background invited everyone to stop and watch the couple take centre stage.

And then there was Matt, her older brother, taking his bride into his arms as they danced a slow waltz. It was very romantic to see two people very much in love holding one another, trapped in their own little bubble. God, Claire couldn't help but glance towards Zack, wondering if perhaps this—what her brother shared—was possible, because dear god, she was falling more in love with this guy every day.

Only when the music reached halfway were guests invited to also join the dance. Without hesitation, Zack got up, grasped Claire's hand, and tugged her along, passing the central activity on the floor and headed outside, where he swung Claire quickly into his arms. It was there Claire held her breath, honouring how he was able to make her feel like rocketing over the moon.

"Are we that different that we have to dance outside away from all the other guests?" Claire muttered, sliding her hands around his neck as they moved slowly, her heels struggling across the grass.

"Course we are, babe," Zack whispered, his hands moving to follow the contour of her hips. "You know we are."

"I love you, you know that?" Claire told him as they rested their foreheads against one another's.

"I do. And I love you more," Zack replied in a hushed tone, leading them further in the dance as they silently stirred in beat to the music.

Love did things to people. Crazy things. It's special when it's authentic. When it did not hesitate ever to stop loving that person.

"Come with me," Claire whispered, breaking the silence between them.

"Where?"

"Upstairs."

"Are you asking me to take my clothes off, Miss Winter?" A cheeky grin formed across his lips.

"Yes."

"I don't object."

Claire smirked, grabbing his hand as she led them back into the hall where guests were still dancing wildly, others still ordering at the bar, and the bride and groom dispersing in their own direction greeting old friends and family. Before they wriggled their way through, she stopped at her mother.

"We're just popping upstairs. The rooms are still booked, right?" she inquired, her implicit meaning also not fooling anyone, especially her mother.

"Yes." Her mother briefly smiled. "This whole venue is hired out. Don't forget about that wild dance you promised with me later on, Claire," she sang before she began to shuffle off, wiggling her hips as she took her husband to the dance floor. She was drunk.

They pushed on, Zack soon taking control as he headed for the staircase. They tackled the first few in a composed manner before leaving the rest in a mad, frenzied manner, laughing as they reached the next floor. With impatience, Zack pushed Claire against the wall, his lips crashing against hers as his hands ran through her hair. His hands then slowly dragged down to her hips before lifting her left leg up against his body as he grinded his pulsating member into that tantalising spot.

Claire tried to suppress a gasp,

acknowledging that they were in earshot of the downstairs reception area. With control, Claire pushed him gently off and tugged on his tie as she pulled him into a room. There she didn't care what he did. Like a hungry tiger, he threw off his suit jacket and pulled off his tie as he prowled after Claire, who took a step back.

His lips met hers in a fiery combat lasting just for a second until Zack pushed Claire onto the bed, flipped her body over, and allowed his hands to take their time flattering every inch of her ass, kneading it like dough.

"You're so fucking...gorgeous." His hoarse, gravelly whisper sent shockwaves all through her body, intensified by the way he dragged her body down the bed, propped her arse in the air, and teased the air in between as he pressed his hardened friend at the rear. It didn't matter that they were fully clothed because dear god, she felt her insides tightening and the urge of exploding was already on the brink of the horizon.

Slowly, she felt him peel back her dress, leaving her naked back exposed and tickled by the air. His lips then made contact starting from her nape all the way down her spine, making it difficult for Claire to remain still. Have no mercy, she thought when he slipped the dress further down her frame, giving centre stage to her Brazilian thong. Each cheek was kissed before he pulled on the elastic string and released it.

"Fuck's sake, Claire. You know how to make a guy feel so hard," he growled in her ear, another wild sensation prickling down below that sent her hormones rocketing with lust. She just couldn't take the anticipation, so she took the control, turning over and sitting up, pressing her lips against his, thirsty to feel his tongue quenching her own. All that while, her dress draped down past her shoulders, leaving her breasts in full view and easy for Zack to squeeze in the palms of his hands. Nor did he leave some out for his mouth, sucking each hardened nipple and eliciting gasps of delight.

His shirt soon came off, then his trousers and boxers. Claire remained in nothing but her thong as she straddled herself in his lap. Her hands moved across the contour of his abs, then around to his back, feeling the movement of his muscles shift as he engulfed her frame into his own.

Growing urgency led to impatience, his hands breaking the flimsy material and immediately entering her hard and fast, hitting her where he knew she would break instantly. Each penetration was sheer bliss, the movement of hands dragging down one another's backs and their hips as they met halfway. Their breathing was erratic. Sweat was inevitable. Positions changed, and sure enough, he had Claire lying on her side as he fucked her sideways, hitting hard and fast. The sweet pain had her succumbing to complete surrender.

Then the ass.

Each thrust. Each fucking thrust. Her hands holding onto for dear life to the bed, each fingertip pressing against the sheets as she felt all of him cater to her satisfaction.

Then major fireworks.

"Oh, god," Claire panted as he slid out of her and rolled onto his back. "God, you're…amazing."

Zack was heavily breathing, too. "You can…speak."

"Dear me." She puffed, laughing a little, but with struggle as she squeezed her eyes closed briefly. "My knickers. You snapped them. How am I supposed to—"

"It'll be our naughty little secret," Zack blurted aloud, heaving as he rolled onto his side to face Claire. His breathing was still a little hectic, but he just couldn't help the next thing that came out from his mouth. "Claire, I need…to tell…you something."

CHAPTER EIGHT

The unwavering bass of the music drumming from downstairs made it impossible for Claire to get a thought in silence. Her eyes lasted only a few seconds to observe Zack's facial expression that flashed contrition before they returned to the side-track of their surroundings. Not that her mind registered or allowed her to completely see it as guilt. Instead, she blatantly ignored whatever words came from out his mouth.

"We better get changed." She smiled weakly, fumbling for her dress off the floor. "Don't want to be caught in the act, do we?" Her attempt at a laugh sounding like a dying cat.

"*Claire.*"

"And god, Zack!" She giggled as she slid the dress across her body. "How am I supposed to walk out without knowing every goddamn second that you tore my knickers? You better hope that there's no one looking *up* those stairs as we go down them."

"*Claire.*"

"I wonder if Mom has persuaded Dad to join her on the dance floor, and he's miserably groaning like he normally does," she scoffed, tugging her one heel back onto her foot. "That would be priceless. So, get ready. C'mon, mister." She slapped her hand playfully several times down onto his chest. Zack remained sitting up, his back hunched forward, guilt sucking on the framework of his face.

"*Claire.*"

"I don't think I'll manage to walk down those stairs, Zack. You might seriously have to carry me because, dear god, does it feel like someone has put the air conditioning on down there," Claire remarked as she slid one of the loose bobby pins back into her hair to secure the odd piece that had escaped cavity in her neat mess. "And—"

"Claire, would you please just listen to me?" Zack interrupted, grasping her thigh as he moved closer down the end of the bed. "This is serious."

"I'm…listening. I am. You just keep repeating my name. So…just spit it out, Zack," Claire muttered, awkwardly getting up and insisting to herself that the expression still attached to his face was nothing more than an attempt to persuade her to get back in bed. "I'm listening, Zack. What is it?"

"I lied."

Claire snorted as she rubbed her right hand across her elbow, feeling the patches of dry skin. She made a mental note to cream her skin later on. Finally, after leaving him with nothing, she replied, "We *all* lie, Zack. One time or another. Only a few do not have the courage to lay down and cover up the truth. Your *point* is? What? Your hair is not a natural black? You lied about not washing up the dishes the other day? Hm?"

"No, no, Claire, that's not—"

"Zack, just *get* changed first. And we talk more—tomorrow morning. Just not now," Claire interjected.

"No, we need to talk about it now, Claire. It's…too important to just allow it to slide," Zack disagreed as he grabbed his boxers, slid them on, and then followed with his trousers. "It's just too damn important." He put on his buckle. "I lied, Claire. About me."

Claire frowned a little, watching as her boyfriend's face took on a guise of solemnness. "Lied how so? What, you lied about your allergies? Your fucking name? What, Zack? What do you mean you lied about you?" Her heart hammered against her ribcage as she felt the room around her suddenly become hotter and denser, that in any second it would engulf her. "God, Zack. What's with all this crap now?

Can't we seriously have a therapy session some other time? It's my brother's day. I—we don't need this. You've got to be pissed or something. How much did you drink?"

"Claire, I'm not pissed. And you need to listen to this now. It's fucked up timing…and well, I should have done this sooner. You're not leaving, nor are you going to give up on us for what I am about to say. Okay? I'm not letting you slip through my fingers because, baby, you know what you feel inside and what I feel inside is true," Zack explained, throwing on his shirt.

"Just spit it out then!" Claire snapped as she flopped herself into the closest corner chair and crossed her arms.

Zack sighed, licking his bottom lip. "My name isn't Zack Chase. I'm Zack Benson—"

"So, you lied about your last name. Big whoop. I don't seriously care, Zack. I love you, and that's all that matters. You can tell me all tomorrow why you chose to lie about that. But for now, let's just go downstairs and—"

"You're not listening, Claire—"

"Well, maybe it's because I don't want to fucking listen, Zack," she cried aloud. "I don't want to hear what you've got to say because I know from the look on your face that there is a slim chance I'll be walking away hand in hand with you. So, yeah, I don't." Groaning a little, she tried to reduce the trembling of her bottom lip.

"Claire," Zack muttered, trying his best to evoke some comfort towards her as he kneeled before her and clasped her hands. "Just…please listen, and I promise you that we will be leaving that door hand in hand." He ran his thumb across her cheek before eventually she nodded. "Does Benson not ring a bell to you?" he asked, his eyes flicking back and forth between her own.

"*No*…why should it?"

"What about where you work?"

Claire's eyes lit up with acknowledgment then. "Okay, I didn't think of that, but what has that got to do with you? Lots of people have the same last names. Doesn't mean you're fucking related."

"Everything, Claire. So much fucking everything." Zack exhaled, allowing one hand to drop away from hers as he used it to anchor his chin. "I'm the CEO, Claire." He dared not for a second to let fall his eyes away from hers. He wanted to see her expression, see her disgust and that anger he knew he deserved, but instead her reaction was far from it.

Claire laughed, shaking her head, "Who put you up to this? *Huh?* Is this some practical joke? Are you okay? Did you hit your head on something along the way?"

"Claire, I'm serious," Zack stressed as he stood up and ran his left hand through his hair.

"I'm not lying. This isn't a joke."

"Zack, I'll give it to you, this is funny. Nice joke. Had me all fired up for no reason. Was that your plan? Wanted some hot, angry, make-up sex? 'Cause if that was all, you should have just asked, although that doesn't mean I'm still not up for it." Claire chuckled, winking at the end as she began to rise.

"Claire, I'm not lying."

"Well, unless you've got concrete evidence, I don't believe a word that comes from out that pretty mouth of yours. Sorry, babe," Claire said, shrugging her shoulders and growing a smirk.

"Here then." He pulled his phone from his back pocket and drummed his fingers across the screen until finally shoving it in front of her. "Do you know who this man is?" He drew her attention towards the man who could be no other human than his father, Elijah Benson. Claire nodded, her humour dying a little as she held his phone.

"Yeah, that's the CEO. I think he retired, though. I know who that is. He was there when I first joined the company. Tough cookie as well."

"Okay then, so what about this?" Snatching the phone out of her hands, he swiped his finger across the screen to the following picture. Claire couldn't even snap back at him for his little cruel seize as he passed her back the phone, projecting yet another picture. Her mouth closed and opened as she registered the old CEO, standing tall and proud alongside his wife and two other men on either side, one who she could see was Zack. *Her boyfriend.*

"*This*…this doesn't make sense," Claire said, shaking her head as her eyes flicked back and forth to the real-life Zack standing before her and the man in the picture. "It—It could just be some lucky photoshop or a mystery doppelganger you never knew about. Ain't no fucking way that is you, Zack. You wouldn't lie about that to me, nor would it make sense."

"It's the truth. That's my family. My dad. I took over the business. I have been for the last couple of years, but I'm invisible in my father's shadow, so very few recognize me. I lied about who I am, Claire, but I'm not lying about how much I feel for you," he said, stepping forward to caress her face.

"Don't touch me!" Claire roared, her fingers still gripping the edges of the phone as she marched back. *"Just don't!"* She shook her head as she bit her inner cheek. "But why? Oh my god." She shook her head, feeling nauseous. "And Graves? You just let him fire me? You. I can't. Why didn't you fucking punish Graves for what he's done? You know all the shit that man has put the department under! And me? Why haven't you done anything? What even is the plan, Zack? Sleep around with me then go back to your big, wide world?"

"No, no, Claire. I have plans for massive changes for this company starting next month. And it killed me not to step up, but I just wanted time to sort it all. I was having trouble in my company. I'll clear your name, get your job back for you. And Claire, no. Don't think like that. I love you, and that was never—"

Claire didn't know what to think, feel, or react. Those three words, "I love you," were starting to feel difficult to register knowing the lies that had surrounded Zack.

"I can't hide why it was initially all done. I need you to know everything," Zack added, running his hands along either side of his arms. "This wasn't done for business. It wasn't planned by the members of the board. There was no official documentation of my absence from the office to intrude into my employees' space. It was between a friend and me. A bet. One that was stupid, but I don't regret it."

"A bet," Claire reiterated, defeat exploring every crevice of her face as she looked down towards the floor.

"It was just to see if I could cope with being normal. Whatever that means. I'll admit you were only involved when we found you had a room to let. You weren't part of it, but you were part of my selfish, egotistical map of thought. You were going to be my fun. But then…I found out you were a challenge, not so easy, and the more I wanted to sleep with you, the more I fell for you. I'm a dick, I know, I should have told you sooner, but I became afraid. As soon as I started falling for you, I believed in this misconception that somehow it would all work out in the end. I forgot for a second that I was a man on top of the world business trade, and I wouldn't have to deal with the consequences to come after," Zack explained, noticing that as he spoke, Claire flinched and pressed her lips together with dismay as she listened to every word. "Claire?"

She looked away, swallowing an uncomfortable taste of bitterness in her mouth. Again, Zack repeated her name aloud. "What do you want me to say, Zack?" she meekly replied, exhaling as she held out his phone. He took it gently, watching as she looked at the photo still intact upon the screen.

"You still love me?" Zack said, uncomfortably shifting his collar.

"Of course I do, Zack, but I just don't know...if I can anymore," she muttered, unable to shift her attention towards his wandering eyes that she could feel were sweeping over her. "I—I just don't if I can handle or even...comprehend what this means anymore. I'm struggling. You lied, Zack." She waved her hands about to emphasise her point. "Although...still...how is that even gonna work between us? I can't see it looking good to my colleagues...nor would I want either of us to feel like I would just have to rely on you—"

"But you wouldn't, Claire. I wouldn't stop you from working. We would be a team—even if your contribution was small—because heck, I don't want you feeling like—"

"But it would. I'd always feel so indebted to you," she blurted, her shoulders slumping forward.

"Claire."

"But why couldn't you just tell me the truth? I've read enough romance books in my life to know that it never usually works out. And now look." Claire frowned, slightly jabbing her hands out to the side of her. "I'm in one myself. You've got to understand that I can't help that nagging voice in the back of my mind telling me that you could be lying. That our entire love affair could be a lie." She held her hand up to stop Zack from butting in. "And then there's that other weak voice, the one I want to trust, telling me I should just follow my heart because it has been through so much with you. Fuck, Zack, you've been there with me when Jonas died. I just—just, honestly don't know what to believe or what to do. I know for sure, though, that I love you. But…I'm gonna need space. Lots of space," she explained, feeling more than ever that her world was slowly falling apart and not a single mechanism could stop the reaction.

"Claire, I love you. Please, just don't. I fucked up. Just give me another chance," he pleaded, grasping her hand that she willingly allowed him to hold. "Baby, please just let me prove it to you. Anything. I'll show you my real world. We'll take it slow if that's what you want. Just don't walk away when you know what we have can never be replaced."

"I…" Claire exhaled. "I need time, Zack."

"Please."

"I just need time to think, Zack. I'm hurt. Really hurt, but…I just…need time to heal. Because, Zack, you fucked up, and now I can't stand to look you in the face without seeing the bold word: liar." She let go of his hand.

"I'm not giving up on you," Zack declared, bringing her forehead against his before pressing a hard, lingering kiss at the centre. "Just don't shut me out. If we could just work this out together…"

"No," Claire said, stepping away. "I need time, and if you love me, you'll allow me this. Just please go. I know you have a home to go back to, so I'll just say something urgent came up. But just please go, Zack."

"Claire."

"Go!" she snapped, jabbing her index finger towards the door. "I don't want to fucking see you, Zack. I don't want to hear from you right now. I need space."

"I can't, and I won't," Zack refused. Claire screamed viciously as she shoved her hands against his chest, trying her best to shift his hefty frame. Tears still failed to make an entrance, holding back until Claire saw fit to do so.

"Please!" she begged, collapsing into his arms in defeat. He engulfed her into an embrace. "P-please."

"I can't, Claire. You need me here."

"I don't want you here." She pulled back and marched away from the man she so desperately loved. "If you won't, I will. Because you're a dickhead, Zack." She found herself crying this time, tears falling like a running tap. "I hate you! I fucking hate you!" She headed towards the door.

"Claire."

"Go! I won't ask again, Zack!" she yelled. "Go!"

"No."

"Well, I am." Then she opened the door, slamming it with effect, leaving the only man she had felt completely alive with standing there in the centre of the room. Zack did not hesitate as he followed hot on her heels, only to find she had not gone far and instead ended up on the opposite side of the wall outside the room, breathing heavily as she closed her eyes.

"Claire, please," Zack muttered, wary of how close he was getting to her. "Don't run. I promise I'll go if you just tell me you won't forget about us. You won't give up, please. That's all I ask."

Claire opened her eyes, redness faintly appearing around the rims as she sniffled. "I can't promise anything, Zack. I really can't." She frantically wiped away the tears upon her cheeks. "I need time."

Zack glanced to the floor, exhaling as he replied, knowing he had little choice but to accept. "I'm not giving up on us, if that's what you need to hear. I'm not lying about how I feel. I'm always here for you, Claire. I won't stop loving you. God, I won't. But I'll try, try to give you space if that's what you desire." Then he dared to step closer, kissing her cheek. She accepted, holding her breath at his gentleness and its reminder of how much she loved this guy. "I love you, Claire." Then he draped his jacket across his shoulders, hesitant to leave at first, but then he turned. With relief and slight dismay, she rolled her body to the side, watching as he walked away. Her heart was screaming inside, banging with all its might against its four walls, wanting to know why she wasn't just shouting after him, jumping into his arms, and playing the weak damsel. He had tried. She had to give him that. He wasn't giving in. And here she was allowing that nagging voice to take control, manipulating all those moments she had with him like fairy tales one would tell their child.

***

CLAIRE

He had left. Simple as that. Downstairs, life went on. The applause, conversation, music, and constant hustling was oblivious to the wreaking havoc that had just occurred between the pair of them. Nobody knew, nobody cared, and there was certainly nobody coming to her rescue.

Standing up was becoming more difficult by the second, even though she was supported by the rose-patterned wall behind her. She could only scoff at its visual impression, ironic how the glistening in her eyes totally made the flowers seem to wilt. Claire truly felt in pain. Her heart gnawed away as the palms of her hands became sweatier, and that fear like she was drowning made her to feel like she was unable to breathe. She just had to get out of here.

Rolling her head to either side, she became aware of the ladies' lavatory at the end of the corridor on the right. Without second thoughts, she rushed in towards the gold-framed mirror, hyperventilating as she gripped either side of the white marble basin. Inhaling and exhaling slowed her to normal respiration—she could breathe. It was only then that her eyes began to search her own reflection, wondering what on earth had made her become so adversely weak. *Idiot*. What was the actual point of crying? It was just so typical. Claire hated this feeling. That vulnerability. Zack had lied. End of. There was nothing either of them could do about that.

Sniffling, she shook her head, encouraging herself to tidy the mess that was staring back at her. With balls of toilet tissue and the odd lather of soap, the end result was a lot more convincing than the initial look she sported that would have easily attracted her mother's attention, even if she was intoxicated.

"Stop being a fucking pussy," she hissed at herself, jabbing her index finger against the transparent surface before sucking in a tunnel of air. "You don't need him. Fuck, you don't need anyone. You've done all right single." Then she exhaled, quickly adjusting the strap of her dress across her bare shoulder.

With a curt nod to her reflection, Claire marched out of the bathroom, nearly colliding with the moving mass that was heading for her. Of course, when she stopped in her path and looked up, her eyes remaining idle upon the figure, it didn't take her long to register it was her mother. A strong scent of wine stained her breath as she asked, "Honey, there you are. Where's Zack?"

At the sound of Zack's name, Claire's stomach clenched, holding its walls tightly together and refusing to deflate. Claire bit down on her bottom lip, threatening the metallic taste of blood to wash into her mouth. "He had to go. Family business. Don't worry, he said for me to tell you he was sorry for his sudden exit. I'm gonna get a taxi and head back to the house, Mom. Tell Dad I'm not feeling well, and if Matt asks, the same," Claire explained, hoping it was enough to curtail her mother from her usual detective mode, but that was very unlikely.

Claire's mother frowned, allowing the door she had been keeping open to swing shut on its hinges, leaving her alone with her daughter. "What's up, Claire?" she inquired, her eyes narrowing into slits as if she were attempting to locate one ant in an army of a dozen. "And why on earth would Zack just leave without at least a proper goodbye? Did something happen?"

Claire sighed. "Mom, nothing happened. He seriously had to go home...I told him to go. It was important. And as for me, I think the alcohol has gone to my head, so I would love if you'd let me slip past. I need to lie down." The lie was a fabrication, but it appeared to work for her mother, who embraced her in her arms.

"Claire, I told you to take your time drinking. And tell Zack he needs to pop around again because I barely got to spend a moment with your fella."

Claire cringed inside, but even if today's turmoil had not occurred, she still would have over her mother's choice of words. Claire nodded even though it was the exact opposite she had in mind.

Eventually she was allowed to scoot past and head downstairs quickly and into the main hall towards the front door. The entrance was lit up by colourful lanterns, a motif to love. She could only detest the sight, tensing a single fist as she headed into the cool breeze.

"Motherfucker," she scoffed, kicking a loose pebble; the background noise of pumping, dynamic music was still prevalent, irritating her even more so that this night could have turned out a little differently.

Why the fuck did he lie? This was the man she had thought could only be capable of lying about the number of his past sexual partners, not lie completely to her face about his identity. She knew it was all too good to be true. Knew that falling in love with him was one huge mistake. But what about everything they went through? There, that tiny voice could only argue for a second before it succumbed to her breaking heart. The one that refused to believe Zack had good intentions. It made the entire picture just so sad.

A deal, though? How was she supposed to react? How was this time she had asked for gonna help? What was she supposed to do? Feel? Think? Where were the answers? Claire just didn't know. There was no instruction manual. No fancy tool she could buy from some

DIY department store and hope to patch up his mess. Instead, it was like taking the wheel blindfolded and wondering when to turn.

CHAPTER NINE

ZACK

Zack knew he had messed up. He regretted his choice of timing, but at the same time he was relieved that the huge amount of weight that had been imposed on his entire shoulders was lifted. Didn't mean it stopped the second stack of weight replacing its absence. He had a long trek ahead of him. The attempt to fix a woman he had broken. He the master and she the feeble puppet.

Home. *What was home now?* That large but lonely complex he called home felt more of a stranger to his heart, lifeless, that flicking on the lights to the central room was just pointless. His place, his bachelor pod, his unnecessarily large-sized penthouse was not home. Not anymore.

He flopped onto the couch, dragging his hands to the remote lying on the side. With a click, automated blinds drew back, allowing the midnight sky in touch with the city's towering skyscrapers to enter his view. His sigh was an echo down a tunnel. It dawned on him…living "normal" wasn't the problem, for he had learned the life of luxury could be deserted; it was the problem of knowing you could be all alone. That was the fear. Money wasn't everything. Clearly.

What Zack loved about alcohol was it didn't talk back, didn't point out the obvious, nor rule his actions as wrong or right, for it just quenched that undying thirst, manipulated the mind into thinking that everything was okay. It became his friend that night, but it also became his enemy; smashed, sharp pieces patterned the floorboards and the lurking stench followed along with.

"Fuck you and fuck you!" he shouted, throwing another bottle against the wall, hooting with laughter as it shattered into tiny pieces behind the sideboard. "I don't fucking care!" Gritting his teeth, he roared with anguish as he shoved all his weight against the sideboard to flip it over, the crash startling his own eardrums. He was broken, his sanity at a loss as he laughed, sliding down the wall onto the floor and slurring incoherent phrases.

After what seemed an eternity just sitting there, light suddenly flooded into the corridor from up ahead, and the lift doors opened, revealing Kyle and a woman. His female companion was dressed head to toe in only a flimsy, silver material that clung against her toned body. At first neither one of them noticed Zack's presence. Kyle spotted the broad-shouldered frame sat in the corner of the room knocking back a bottle of beer out of the six-pack placed beside him.

"I can't tonight," Kyle whispered to the woman, shaking his head to apologise. "Some other time. You have my number." He pecked her cheek despite her displeased expression as he waved her off. Drawing his hands into his pockets, Kyle called over, "So what are you doing, buddy? I see you've made yourself quite a mess by the looks of it."

Zack didn't reply, only shrugged his shoulders before taking another exasperated sip.

"What happened? Didn't you have that wedding…?" Kyle persisted, trying to get some sort of response from his friend, who remained mute. "I wouldn't really be sitting there. There's broken glass all around you. You could cut yourself, and we wouldn't want to be taking a trip down to A&E, would we? C'mon, Zack. Just get up."

Zack kicked his legs further out, shifting glass where his feet slid along the floorboard. "Shame about that woman. She looked a'right." He smirked, tipping back the bottle.

Kyle shook his head, snatching the bottle

from his hand. "Fuck's sake, Zack. You're pissed as anything."

"*Oh, I know.*"

"What the fuck happened, Zack? Is this something to do with your dad?" Kyle said.

"Ha! That fuckerrr? He was the one…*fuuucking* up my business, so *yeah,* you could say he's a problem," Zack slurred, lifting himself awkwardly off the floor and then rubbing his face. "Fuck, why you have to mention him for, though? Just give me back the bottle and I'll do you some peace when I head off to bed."

"It's got something to do with that Claire, hasn't it? You told her."

Zack froze, frowning as he snatched back the bottle. "Fuck off," he spat.

"Oh, and this is gonna help. Wow, first medal goes to Zack. Grow some balls. You ain't for this loved-up shit, as you used to say. But now when the real deal comes, you're being an ass," Kyle argued back, following his friend, who slouched over to the kitchen.

"Man, if I wanted this lecture, I would have gone to my mother. Just shut up," Zack grumbled, waving his hand about as he gripped his fingers around the bottle's neck.

"I'm just saying. Just—"

"Yeah, well, don't," Zack interrupted, shaking his head. "I don't want to hear it, Kyle. God, just leave it, all right?" He turned around

115

to face his friend with frustration. "Don't heckle me, okay? I know you've got my back, but I just don't need it tonight. I'll be all right in the morning. Let me just drink."

"Fine," Kyle replied, holding up his hands in surrender. "Fine."

"Just have a drink with me," Zack said, knocking his bottle against the counter's surface. "Grab yourself one. It's the least you can do considering you'll only be dry-humping a pillow tonight."

"Fuck off, Zack." Kyle smirked briefly before tipping back a bottle that Zack handed over. It became quiet then between the pair as neither said a word and instead accepted that it was nice to just be in the other person's company.

***

CLAIRE

Claire sat on the edge of her old bed, glancing around her room at the old memories. Several cute, vibrant stickers stuck against one side of the wall reminded her of that phase she went through like every girl, wanting to collect as many as possible and decorate any little thing they could grasp their hands on. Then the stuck-on-with-blue-tac pictures of old celebrity crushes and trending fashion items had home on another. The majority there reached into the spectrum of late teen, with the library of schoolbooks, old bottles of perfume, and that old leaflet she had taken back with her from a concert. Her room was almost like a museum, untouched and holding sentimental value that her mother would always go on about. At least it distracted her. Gave her some sort of relief. God, all she wanted to do was have a good night. Come back home and lie on this bed with his arms around her. Then she found herself reconstructing it entirely in her mind, drawing every little detail and every word that came out their mouths.

"I enjoyed tonight," Zack said as his arms cradled her closer and the growing smile progressed on her lips. "I gotta say your mom is quite the dancer, too."

Claire snorted. "Say that to her face and she'd make a shrine just for you."

Zack chuckled. "But on a serious note..." His laughter ceased. "I like your family. They're...great folks."

"And that's why I came out perfect," Claire inserted, shifting in his arms to face him before pecking him on the nose. Zack's smirk went on for days as they said nothing for a moment, only appreciating what was before them.

"You know," Zack began as he rested his

forehead against hers, "Claire Winter, I've fallen right for you. And...if you wanted an old wooden cabin by the lake built by hand, just pass me the hammer, love. I'd build..." He paused for a second as he kissed her lips in between each word. "Biggest..." Another pause. "Greatest—"

"I get it, Romeo." She chuckled lightly, tickled by the brush of his five o'clock shadow against her skin. "I get it. You love to make me cringe, don't you?"

"Always."

Claire shook her head as she pressed her lips together, too happy for words—not even that she could manage one when Zack suddenly sat up and began shifting his hips deliberately side to side, prompting the bed to squeak. She laughed, grabbing one of the pillows and smacking it against the side of his torso. "Ssssh. God, Zack. My parents' room is right next door," she hissed with embarrassment as her cheeks burned.

"Boy, these springs move. Hey, don't you worry, baby. I'm just getting them all worked up." The famous, mischievous grin crossed his face as he did not stop for a second from fidgeting on the squeaky bed until eventually he leaned on down and ensnared her lips. And mother-of-baby-lambs, it was a snog. Her fingers chased towards his waistband as she felt him dig into the core of her burning centre.

Laughter overtook the image but then dispersed out of sight as a wash of grey clouds snatched it away, and soon Claire was brought back to where she was, sitting in the dark pits of her room staring out into space.

Zack Benson. That was the man she'd been cooped up with. But was he still the man she had fallen in love with?

CHAPTER TEN

She tossed and turned all through the night, unable to catch a wink of sleep as a suffocating blanket of today's occurrence romped around in her mind, forcing her to dwell on it. It must have taken her till around half four in the morning after plodding down to her parents' kitchen for a glass of water that she snuck off into a drowsy state, exhaustion finally eating her up. As for this morning, Claire was weak and couldn't understand why she was downstairs at eight o'clock, sitting at the head of the kitchen table and barely able to lift the cup of tea that rested between her clasped hands. She should still be in bed like her parents, who had come home around three in the morning.

As for Zack, she had received about a dozen text messages all through the night enticing her to answer. No wonder she had so much trouble sleeping last night. The glare of the screen projecting upon the white ceiling acted strangely on her imagination as some sort of Morse code, keeping her brain wildly active.

"Hey, pet." The sudden appearance of her father entering the kitchen startled her, his faded green t-shirt and long blue pyjama bottoms a familiar sight. "You're up early. Couldn't sleep? Your mother is snoring her head off, so I couldn't dare stay one more second in that room." He chuckled as he put the kettle on.

Claire attempted a smile, but the concern written upon her father's face said it all. "What's up, sweetheart? Everything okay? I mean, it was a little strange, you leaving so early last night, but your mother told me it was because Zack had some family emergency. Is he all right today?"

"He's fine, Dad. I'm fine. Just tired, that's all," Claire lied, knowing all too well that her father's suspicions would not be relieved. She just wasn't a good liar today. Pouring the hot water into the mug and stirring the teabag until a vortex appeared, he walked over, sat down, and still didn't breathe a word, making Claire more uncomfortable. He was using the Dad stare, that very same one he'd use on her as a kid until she blurted out the truth if she stole that cookie or those several times she wouldn't admit who was bullying her in primary school.

It was such a manipulative device that not

long after she sighed, admitting the veracity of the problem. "Okay, Dad. You win…it's Zack."

Her father's brows lifted up, the second stage in the Dad stare that she recognised as the look of relief. "What did the chap do? I thought everything was all sunshine and rainbows between you two. Even your brother said he liked the man. And well…to be honest, petal, I could see myself liking him. So what happened?"

Claire let out an exasperated sigh, scratching her wrist lightly as she began. "He lied…he fucked up, Dad. And I'm stuck because I don't know what to believe. I just don't know where our relationship stands anymore."

Andy frowned a little as he appeared to think it over, the tiny cogs working hard before eventually he replied, "What did he lie about, sweetheart?" The steam from his mug wavered in the atmosphere as it sat undisturbed.

"About him. About who he is. Everything," Claire muttered, shrugging her shoulders as she slid her index finger around the diameter of her cup. "His name isn't Zack Chase. He's Zack Benson. The significance of Benson in that he's my boss. The master behind the corporation I work for. Only, here's the fucked-up part. The part I'm struggling with is he did all of this because of a bet with a friend. A bet that makes it extremely difficult for me to believe that perhaps he feels the same as I do for him,"

Claire finished, feeling a little better for getting it all out into the open to the only man in her life who could never break her heart.

"Well," Andy swallowed, blinking several times as he shuffled uncomfortably in his chair. "So he is the company's leader then? And he…has been…"

"It just doesn't matter anymore because I think it's over between us and—"

"Hey, hey," Andy interrupted, leaning forward eagerly as he shook his head. "No, no. Honey, as much as I would love to kick him where he would scream the high notes, I just want to take a minute—or rather you to think what you're saying. I know this is all so bizarre. But honestly…" He paused as he clasped his hand over hers. "Do you honestly feel he is lying? Lying about how he feels? I mean, he is a complete fool for lying in the first place about all of it, but…Claire, he came here with you. He met me and your mother. Now, I don't want you to feel like I'm vouching for the guy because I'm not. You're my baby girl, and no one gets away with murdering your heart. But there is a chance that this man isn't lying that he loves you."

Claire slid her right hand across her forehead before dragging it through the parting of her hair, the stiffness of yesterday's hairspray tangling it around her fingers. "I know. I know. But it's just so hard. He's part of the reason why I lost my job. He let that happen. He must have known. And then…the whole lie about himself, how can you trust someone you don't really know? I just don't know."

Andy sat back, finally bringing his mug to his lips, taking a brief sip, then drawing back as he sighed, "I just can't believe he's the big boss. Like, that's huge. And your mother doesn't know?" He looked directly in her eyes.

"No."

"Damn."

"What do I do, Dad?"

Andy ran his hand across his chin. "Honey, I'd do what you feel is best. If this was some ordinary chap, I'd probably go over there and tell him how it is, but this is a man with influence and power. I don't know what he could do. Looking back yesterday, he seems decent, and like I said, I very much could see the happiness between you two. But now this is all under a different light, and I can't tell you what to do."

"I know," she said, attempting a short smile. "Thanks, Dad. You won't tell Mom, will you? Not until all of this blows over?"

"No, honey." Andy shook his head. "Come here." He opened his arms for an embrace. Claire got up and slouched around the kitchen table until she flopped into her father's arms. "You always attract the weird 'uns, don't you, Claire Winter?" he remarked with a slight chortle.

Claire hugged her father as she said, "You know me, Dad. I'm *not* normal."

As Claire drew back, the arrival of her mother was evident by the state of the woman standing at the door; messy, recently dyed hair stuck against her face, dried saliva upon the pink collar of her pyjama top, and the exhaustion beneath her eyes.

"What are you two up to?" She yawned, hobbling over to the sink and grasping a glass from the rack. "God, my back kills. And why on earth did I wake up? I don't know."

"Well, *love*," Andy said in return. "You were the one drunk off your head on that dance floor. I'm pretty sure half the guests left because of you—Matt even went off to his honeymoon an hour early."

"Cheeky bugger," she scoffed before she drank back the pint of water.

"Well, it did sound like a tornado had ripped through the house last night when you two came back home. What were you doing, Mom? Wrecking the joint?" Claire pitched in, grateful this household was always able to put a smile on her face.

"Oh, ha ha ha, Claire," she spluttered, forgetting she had a mouthful of water. "God, I need some paracetamol. Andy, grab me some from the cupboard above you." She flicked her finger out to point directly towards the spot she'd described. Her husband chortled as he stood up and opened the cupboard door.

"Can you believe my son is married?" she blabbered to herself. "Claire, we're just waiting on you now. And then it will be the question of who will have grandchildren first."

Claire winced, looking down into her cup, thankful for her father's awareness to the situation as he chipped in, directing his wife off course. "Honey, here, pop these in your gob and go get yourself in the shower. You don't exactly smell lovely." He handed over two pills and ushered her with his other hand towards the door.

"Oi!" she exclaimed. "I'll have you, Andy." Then she turned towards Claire. "Honey, I thought we could do some shopping before you head off. I'm not taking no for an answer, so go get yourself ready and we'll be off. Andy, you're taking us. So don't even think for one minute that you'll be sitting out in that garage of yours." She turned to her husband, who was drinking back more of his cup of tea. "And as for our recently hitched son, Andy, send him a text message to remind him to phone us when he's safely off the plane." And there was the normalcy of her mother. It would be difficult to think she had been drunk last night if it weren't for the state of her appearance this morning.

***

As much as it prompted Claire to feel a little satisfied, the two bags of clothes she'd purchased just weren't enough to maintain that level as soon as the sight of the two-storey flat came into view. She was a little hesitant to get out of the taxi, which irritated the driver, who kept fidgeting and glaring into the rear mirror to see if Claire was going to move. Nonetheless, she remained in the backseat, not moving a muscle.

"Err, miss?" the driver said, clearing his throat. "We're here."

Claire blinked several times, acknowledging the frustration laced through his tone and the way his hands squeezed the steering wheel from the bell alerts echoing off his phone. She preferred the last driver who had driven them down to her parents', even though he might have been a little irksome at times. At least she suspected he might have allowed her to uncomfortably sit it out and tackle her feelings surrounding Zack.

With her suitcase out of the boot and the two designer bags sat before her feet, Claire eyed the building up and down as if she had never seen it in her entire life. She knew she couldn't stand there all day, so with much encouragement from the crowding dark, grey clouds in the sky, Claire began the daunting journey to her apartment.

Thankfully, she found no Zack. Nor did it appear he had even stepped foot in the place because his room was preserved like a museum artefact. Claire didn't feel like packing, didn't feel like eating, even though it read on the kitchen's clock that it was past lunch and the rumbling in her stomach begged for food. Instead, she chucked on a romcom, threw on her night gown, and cuddled with some old teddy she had stuffed at the bottom of her wardrobe.

Then she just sat on the sofa, not even pressing play at the title screen as it replayed the prime scenes of the film repeatedly. This was not what she wanted to do. She didn't want to be sitting on the sofa feeling sorry for herself and dwelling over one guy. Instead, she wanted to do the exact opposite, just like that one rare empowering character she had come across: Miranda Elliot. What a badass she was, went through tough relationships and each one she'd not shed a tear, only go home, put on her best makeup and dress, and wear it around the house. She wouldn't go anywhere, just simply stalk in the house and feel that she owned that motherfucker; no guy could lay a finger on her.

"Fuck this," she spat, heaving herself off the couch and switching off the telly. Claire marched down into the hallway, slamming open her bedroom door as she ran through, then rummaged in her wardrobe attempting to find the sexiest thing she owned. She wasn't going to mope around; she was going to be like Miranda and prove that this guy couldn't get to her. So, without wasting a second, she spent an hour and a half dolling herself up in the shoes, the lingerie, the makeup, and the skimpy red dress that flashing enough cleavage from its daring neckline. And then she rushed into the kitchen and grabbed the bottle of wine, mimicking Miranda's actions, and drank that motherfucker like it was last supply in the entire world.

With the bottle still in her hand, she sashayed her hips into Zack's room, picking up the tossed shirt on the floor by the pads of her fingers as if to say it was contaminated and throwing it into the wastebasket in the corner of the room.

"Fuck this!" she yelped, throwing her hands into the air and growling to herself as she kicked off the quilt from his bed. "You bastard." She began throwing the pillows off the bed. Old sex stained the bed, spurring her on towards the sickening thought that all of it could have been to manipulate her. "Nothing is real!" She was not at all concerned if the neighbours could hear her shout from the paper-thin walls.

Exhaustion was the only line of attack that could make her surrender. Why on earth she chosen Zack's room? His smell coated every inch of the bed and the exact same radiating warmth she'd feel when encased in his arms, felt real and alive from the shirt she clutched in her hands. Just why did he lie? Good God, why couldn't she believe he was swearing the truth? She loved him. There was no denying that. And that was what hurt so much. Her dad was right; there was nothing that anyone else could do to solve the matter. It had to be her. But what was the right answer?

She must have fallen asleep because she awoke from a series of knocks on the front door. Groggily, she glanced towards the bedside clock, realising she had slept at least two hours. Whoever kept knocking pushed her to go answer; otherwise the neighbours might have another reason to complain.

"All right, all right, all right, I'm coming!" she groaned, weakened by those blissful hours of sleep she had. Eventually, she reached the door, making no effort to ensure she was in the best state to be seen. Claire opened the door, scrunching her eyes as she struggled against the adjustment of light. Only now she wished she had never opened the door seeing the man she was in turmoil over standing there looking fresh in a new change of clothes.

"No," she hissed, pushing the door in his face, yet Zack successfully barricaded the effort. "Let go of the door, jackass." Her drowsiness dispersed at the awakening of realisation that he was indeed here.

"Claire, no," Zack objected, standing his ground and barely using any of his own strength against Claire's weak push. "I gave you time. I gave you a day. I told you I'm not going anywhere. Fuck, Claire. You didn't answer any of my messages. I was worried that something happened to you."

"That's not your job anymore," Claire scoffed.

"It is."

"It is not."

Zack sighed, biting down on his tongue as he rolled his head to the right. "We're not doing this, Claire. Just let me in and we can sit and talk about this. You need me with you."

"No, I don't. I've decided I don't need you anymore. I don't want no lying man. So you can fuck off and go shag some other woman." She jabbed her finger in the air at him. "That's all you are. Ain't it? A man whore! You used me for sex! That's all you are! Man fucking whore!"

"Claire, you're not thinking straight. You've been drinking." Zack attempted to reason with her, but she just continued to cut him off.

"Fuck you!" she hissed bitterly. "I'm done. We're done." She waved her hands about as she shook her head.

Zack looked down the hallway and back to his feet. His eyes lingered there for a second before suddenly he pushed, breaking back the door and forcing himself inside. With his arms out wide, he ensnared her into his embrace, cooing against her ear, "It's okay, baby. It's okay. Ssssh. I'm here." He kicked the door shut before guiding her further into the apartment. Claire was hopeless in fighting back, too tired and weak.

"C'mon, over here," he muttered, aligning her in front of the couch where gently he helped her sit back. "C'mon, Claire. That's it, sweetie," he encouraged as his fingertips caressed the left surface of her cheek. "I'm not going anywhere. Just sit here and close your eyes if you need to."

"I don't want you here…" Claire moaned, spluttering a little as she hid her face in the cushions. "Just…go…away." She mumbled incoherently through the pillow before it was summarily removed and she found herself lying on top of his thigh.

"Claire, I'm so sorry…I fucked…up…so bad." She heard him speak, although the natural fatigue taking a toll upon her body made it difficult to pay attention. "But I swear, we'll make this work. I promise." Another whisper of words as she felt herself drift slowly back to sleep. "We'll make this work." The final words that managed to project through lay in her sleepy mind.

***

Claire's sensitive nose caught the scent of sizzling bacon, impelling her to open her eyes and catch the thieving culprit who had taken out the packet from the fridge.

Lifting herself off the sofa, her attention shifted straight towards Zack, who was mindlessly unaware she had awoken. His tongue was sticking out the right corner of his lips as he meticulously prodded the fork into the pan, seeming afraid to burn it to a crisp. He leant in closely to inspect its state. She didn't say anything at first, her head was still a little drowsy, but it was obvious he had not left.

Her back was killing her as she attempted to stand up. She kicked her heels out the way before hobbling over to the kitchen. Swallowing what little saliva she could manage from a parched throat, she spoke bitterly. "What are you still doing here?"

Zack turned off the gas dial, sliding the bacon onto the slice of bread placed conveniently adjacent on the counter next to the oven. "I heard a greasy breakfast is the best cure for a hangover," he replied, ignoring her statement as he continued to squeeze a dollop of ketchup onto the bacon then finished it altogether with the second slice of bread on top. "Here, eat this. And I did put some water by the side of you. Paracetamol is also there if you need it." He cut the sandwich into two neat triangles.

Claire pulled a grimace, her rumbling stomach arguing otherwise. "I don't need you babysitting me, nor do I want you here. Need I remind you I told you I wanted time?"

"First, bullshit," Zack began, tearing off a strip of kitchen roll. "You got pissed last night, Claire. And secondly, I am not sitting in my fucking lonely-ass penthouse moping about when I should be redeeming myself and being right here with you, proving to you that I'm not a liar about this relationship. Call me selfish for not giving you your time, but I can't let you slip through my fingers."

"What? You want an orchestra of violins? I'd rather you were there than here. I can't even stand the sight of you. I hate your face," Claire snapped back, then she took the plate and shuffled back over to the sofa.

Zack laughed bitterly. "And yet you take my bloody bacon sandwich. I think you do need me here then."

"I'm hungry, and it's my bacon. Now, just fuck on off back home, Zack," Claire grumbled through a mouthful of food. Zack stalked over, taking the spot right next to her, where he crossed his arms in protest.

"Go away," Claire gasped, shoving his shoulder away. "Can't you take a hint?"

"And can't you take a hint?" Zack sneered, lifting his eyebrows up. "I ain't moving. We need to talk this out properly. And you can keep saying you don't need me, but I know you do."

Claire groaned with frustration. "I'm hating you so much right now." Then she took another uncomfortable mouthful of bacon, hunger being more important to her than her ability to argue.

"Look," Zack said, slapping his hands on his knees. "I know this is difficult. It's more fucked up considering this wasn't a professional tactic and instead was cooked up between me and my friend...but Claire..." He shifted his body slightly to face her directly. "It didn't centre around just sleeping with you. That was just me being a fucking dick. As soon as I got to know you, I realised it was more than that. And then, yes, there was another good, valid reason for this. My company was being fucked about with. So I had to sort out that, too. Another thing I shall explain to you."

She didn't say anything.

Zack moaned in annoyance, flopping his head back as he massaged his temple. "You're one stubborn woman, Claire. What more can a man do to prove his affection?" Then he slid his hand towards his nose, pinching the bridge as he shut his eyes, refusing to emit another word.

They both sat in silence, Claire reluctant to finish off her sandwich as she placed it on the coffee table. Why was she so suddenly at a loss for words? Why wasn't she standing in her own corner? How had she become so quiet that she lost her prevailing argument? Last night, she had given up on the idea of a relationship between them, she had vouched for her independence, but now sitting there, the tables had turned. After all, he was here. Wasn't that making an effort? Wasn't that a sign? Goddamit, why couldn't her emotions just be clearer? He didn't have to be here, and if he was lying, surely it wouldn't bother him.

She sighed, the first sound of activity breaking the silence between them. "I'll give that to you, you are here," Claire muttered, awakening Zack's attention.

His eyes opened, and he slid his hand away as he glanced at the white ceiling. "I'm so sorry, Claire. You're not stubborn. You have every right to be mad. I lied to you, and so I know, I know, it makes our chances slim. I shouldn't have lied. I should have been honest—"

"I know. And I can see you're trying to make amends. It's just hard, Zack. I really, really loved you," Claire interrupted, her tone sad and dismal.

Zack sat up. "Do you still love me?"

Claire clenched her hands together as she looked down to her lap. "I-I…"

Zack cut her off as he scooted closer and cupped her cheek in his hand. "Please don't tell me this doesn't make your heart flutter," he whispered before dangerously taking a risk to kiss her lips. Fortunately, she willingly responded, sliding her hands around his neck as their lips kneaded together gently, rekindling an old love. The taste. It was so pure. So sweet. He was attentive. His hands respectfully remaining laced through her hair. He was the one to pull back.

With their foreheads resting against one another for support but also not to disturb the sudden interaction, Claire could only close her eyes in response to the throbbing sensation of her lips.

"Of course I still love you, Zack," she admitted aloud to her heart. "I didn't mean what I said last night…I still love you." She caressed her thumbs against the bristly surface of his jaw. He pulled her into an embrace, resting his head in the crevice of her neck, holding on tight. She held him, suffering the blinks of tears and fully intoxicated by that familiar scent—Zack's.

She didn't want to let go. Didn't want to feel that penetration of aching in her heart.

Then he spoke and broke the lingering silence. "I'll give you time if that's what you need just as long as you say you won't give up on me," Zack offered, pulling back and wiping away the trail of a tear meandering down her right cheek. "Two weeks. For both of us. To get our shit together. Then you get to decide. Not me. You."

Claire croaked, holding back a flood of tears as she nodded her head desperately. "I promise,

I promise." Then she was the one to pull him in close, interlocking their lips in a hopeless yearning for a second or two before they broke apart. "Thank you," she exhaled, shaking her head as she looked down. "Why couldn't this be easier? I don't want to wait. I crave—"

"Ssssh," Zack interjected, clasping her hand. "Two weeks, baby. That's all it is. I need to respect that you need time. I've put a lot on your shoulders, so you need the time to think it over. If you know that you love me, then the end of that deadline will come sooner than you think, baby." He pressed a hard kiss against the surface of her knuckles.

Claire sniffled. "I told my dad. He knows, Zack. I had to," Claire confessed, searching for any sign of disgust, yet his frank response was understanding.

"I don't care," he replied, shaking his head. "Don't feel bad. Your father has every right to hate me—"

"He doesn't hate you, Zack. Far from it. He's right...I shouldn't give up," Claire said, squeezing Zack's hand.

Zack offered a smile, squeezing her hand with encouragement. "Two weeks. That's all. Think it over and this will soon be nothing but a bad dream."

"I promise."

"I love you so much, Claire."

That was a reconstruction.

***

"What? You want an orchestra of violins? I'd rather you were there than here. I can't even stand the sight of you. I hate your face," Claire snapped, then she took the plate from his hands as she shuffled back over to the sofa.

Zack laughed bitterly. "And yet you take my bloody bacon sandwich. I think you do need me here then."

"I'm hungry and it's my bacon. Now, just fuck off back home, Zack," Claire grumbled through a mouthful of food. Zack stalked over, taking the spot right next to her, where he crossed his arms in protest.

"Go away," Claire gasped, shoving his shoulder. "Can't you take a hint?"

"And can't you take a hint?" Zack sneered, lifting his eyebrows up. "I ain't moving. We need to talk this out properly. And you can keep saying you don't need me, but I know you do."

Claire groaned with frustration. "I'm hating you so much right now." Then she took another uncomfortable mouthful of bacon, hunger more important to her than her ability to argue.

"Hate's a strong word," Zack commented as he sat back.

"Good, because I do."

"No, you don't, Claire."

"Yes, I do," Claire spat back.

"Well, blimey. If you can make your mind up

on something over the course of two nights, then you must be fucking out of your mind. You don't hate me, Claire. The alcohol has been talking to you," Zack said with vexation.

"Fuck you, Zack," Claire hissed, throwing her plate onto the coffee table. "Don't go telling me how and what I should feel. You're the one who fucked up."

"Fuck me. Claire, you're being so irrational right now. And yes, I get it. I don't deserve any sympathy, but I'm here, am I not? I'm here proving to you I want us. I'm not being a dick and leaving you to mope around. I want you, Claire. I'm owning up to my mistake. I'm asking for a second chance," Zack said bitterly as he ran his hands through his hair without grace. Then he sighed, his eyes floating towards the ceiling. "Fuck's sake, Claire. I love you. Is that not enough?"

He grabbed an adjacent pillow and covered his face.

"You sound like a fucking walrus." Claire frowned, snatching the pillow away from his face.

"Well, I'd always wondered why I had big tusks and lived in the fucking Arctic Ocean," Zack replied with a hint of sarcasm as he adjusted his watch around his right wrist.

Claire looked over to him with disdain. "Not funny."

"Not trying to be. Now, let's cut to the

chase," Zack stated as he stood up impatiently. "Tell me now how you want me to prove this to you. Honestly." He motioned with his hands. "What, Claire? Just tell me. I'll do anything."

"I asked for time," Claire grumbled, turning her eyes away to rest elsewhere.

A pinch of silence loitered, that it left Claire still hanging on tight to the patch of wall she was trying ever so hard to focus on, whereas Zack stood where he was, vexed, shown by the several times his hands had ran through his hair.

"Time," he reiterated heavily, relaxing his hand on his hip. "Why isn't this a better alternative? Huh?" He began after a second's pause. "We can talk it out. Bullshit with all this 'I need time.' How on earth is that going to help? If anything, you're just going to be put off more. I know—"

"Zack!" she barked, cutting him off from his rant as she launched to her feet. "Stop! Just stop!" She paced around to other end of the coffee table and back to her initial spot. "After that night, you said you'd give me time. And— and you said all the time I desired. But—but you're here!" Her tone croaked a little. "How on earth do you think I'm able to process this…this…situation so quickly? Huh? Am I just supposed to sleep it over one night and think yeah, everything's good the next day? What gives you the right to come in here and tell me we should talk about it? Huh?"

"I'm—Claire, I just can't see why you don't want to talk it through now!" Zack snapped back, lifting his hand to his forehead.

"I just don't, okay!" Claire snarled, clasping her hands harshly around her cheeks. "You lied, Zack. And you keep telling me you love me, but my mind is in a battle of contradiction at the moment. I need time to adjust, to think. I thought you understood that after that night." Slapping her hands together, she paced around the room. "Eurgh, why are you so difficult? Why did you have to fucking lie? Why did it have to me? Why, why, why?" she groaned, shaking her head. "Why you? Why couldn't it still be Jason? I used to absolutely adore that guy. So why did you have to come along? Damnit!" Cradling herself into a hug, she rested her head against the wall closest to the front door.

"Claire, c'mon," Zack encouraged gently as he went on over to her. "You don't mean that." He comforted her, resting his hand on the wall to hold himself up steady. "We're good together, me and you. We were fighting against this love for ages, and look what it did—it only brought us together. Don't tell me you regret falling in love with me. Don't say that because I don't know for the love of Mars what I'll do if—just god, Claire. I'm sorry. Fuck."

Claire remained where she was, sniffling. Her reply was garbled by emotion. "I don't know anymore, Zack. I don't even know if I know you." She sniffled again. "God, I hate you so much."

"No, no, Claire." Zack placed a hand on her shoulder, disrupting her from her moment of silent whimpering. "Please, I love you so much, baby—"

Hastily, she pivoted on her toes and heckled whatever he was about to say with his lips on high alert with the taste of her own. It was no peck, but a full-on kiss locked in an embrace, her hands dragging him with yearning, closer towards her level, and his control, cautious, at the unexpected interaction. "God, I hate you," she moaned.

Claire tugged him along, yesterday's dress rising up her thighs with the action. With his bottom now back on the sofa, she leaped into his lap, stripping back his top as their lips remained in a fiesta. Her lips sucked on his before biting down on his bottom lip playfully. And her hands remained interested elsewhere with his hardened member, teasing it through the denim material of his jeans. Growing urgency took over as she began to kiss his chest, her nails clawing down his shoulders and the shameful wetness at the centre of her knickers. All the while, Zack was wary, his hands remaining solely resting on her back.

"Shit, shit, shit," she cursed suddenly, pulling back and clenching her eyes together. "No, no, what am I doing? What are we doing?" She complained aloud as she hopped off his lap and ran her hands through her nestled, tangled hair. "Oh, god! Why do I have to be so fucking hormonal with you? And you!" She jabbed her finger at him. "Why do you have to be so intoxicating? Eurgh, I'm such a mess!"

"Claire—"

"No!" she snapped, cutting him off. "Get up! Now! Two weeks, Zack." She grabbed his top with fury as she guided him to the front door. "Two weeks."

"Two weeks for what?" Zack said, finally awakening from his daze.

Pushing him into the corridor, she threw his top back at him. "Give me two weeks. Nothing less. Two weeks."

"What? Time?"

"Yes, I need to think." Then she slammed the door before falling to her knees in a flood of tears.

Some talk that was.

CHAPTER ELEVEN

CLAIRE

"And then…" Claire broke into tears even before she could manage her sentence as she fell into Darren's arms. It was Tuesday, and for the past hour, she had been cooped up in Darren's apartment as she went over every last detail in relation to her turmoil with Zack Benson.

"God, I just can't believe it," Darren confessed as he rocked Claire in his arms to soothe her broken heart. "Nor can I get over the fact he is our big boss. I wouldn't have guessed, but I can definitely see him as that now."

"I'm sorry for putting this on you, Darren." She sniffled, gently pulling back, knowing her behaviour had been right depressing, especially since this man had been through so much. "I know you're still—"

"Hey, hey," Darren interjected, swiping tears away from her cheeks. "Claire, don't. I'm glad you're telling me. I need to get back to some normalcy around here. And baby, you'll need me for all the advice in the world." Her friend offered a warm smile, reminding her just for that odd second that the old Darren was back, safe, from whatever chest he had been locked in deep down in the pits of his heart. It didn't have a lasting effect; from her viewpoint she could still see that tired, defeated man who had lost the man he'd loved.

"And yesterday?"

Claire exhaled. "Just thank god I don't have a job there, right?" She snorted.

"So, what happened Sunday then?"

"Well, of course, I got pissed. He shows up. I wake up Monday and he's still there and we argued and then suddenly I was the one trying to get him into bed. As if shit wasn't bad enough as it was," Claire explained with utter remorse, her need to cry weakened.

Darren smirked slightly. "I'd always said you were a horny bastard."

Claire shook her head with a slight smile, loving that she knew her friend could always make her smile. Darren clapped his knees softly as he inhaled. "So…" He pushed the air back out his lungs. "What are you going to do?"

"Honestly?"

"Yeah, you've said two weeks. So, what?"

Claire pulled up one of her socks, ignoring the question at first, knowing she did not have the answer. She could only shrug in return.

"Well, here," Darren began, leaning forward off his armchair to stir his green tea with another whisk of the teaspoon. "You have options, so that's one good thing. You can walk away or you can stay." Claire could only glance at the pink blanket he was sitting on, feeling numb to even wanting to bother to listen. "He has lied. He's been a dick. He did probably have intentions to just sleep with you as a bonus but—" Darren stopped, a deliberate pause to study Claire's fed-up expression. "He has learnt to grow. He's became attached to you. And when J—" Darren swallowed, clenching his eyes briefly. "On the night of Jonas's...death..." The struggle was evident in his second pause. "He was there for you. If he...didn't love you, he had every chance to walk away."

Claire reached over to squeeze his hand, seeing the utter effect of despair and loss towards mentioning "his" name. Darren returned the gesture before he continued, "Claire, don't make a mistake. Don't be stubborn. We don't...control time. So..." He swallowed back another mouthful of tears. "Just do what is right."

"I love you," she said as she brought his hand to her lips, her touch grazing his knuckles.

"I love you too, my baby."

Claire embraced him into her arms, then she pressed a kiss to his cheek before she whispered, "He's always here with you. Don't forget that."

***

Tuesday late evening in an apartment that felt bare was disturbingly depressing.

Flicking the meatball with her fork, she could only sigh. Two weeks. Two weeks to get her mind around all of this. What did it mean for them? What would it mean if she did go back? What would it mean to their relationship? After all, he was a billionaire. A man, who she had thought didn't know how to wash up or hoover because he was a couch potato, not that he had a maid cleaning up after his ass. It did indeed feel like she was missing the final piece of the puzzle. Did she even know him then? Or was it different?

Darren spoke convincingly, too. Now, she had to really think.

CHAPTER TWELVE

Sweat clung to their skin. The pads of their fingertips stuck to one another as the rocking motion endured. Heavy, carnal moans of their shared desire ran wild. Arousing to the ears, a mind fuck, all building up; a second over and it would explode like a fizzy can of pop, disturbed.

Cries of ecstasy, stimulated by the kneading of his hands upon her breasts, his lips replacing their position to suck and tug on the pink, aroused part. All the while, her hands searched the flat, horizontal surface of his back. Clawing her nails down, resulting in zig-zagged patterns of raw redness.

Inside, the tip of his dick ramming against her core generated titillating waves through her bottom yet lingered more so in the bay of her stomach. Then without surprise, the piercing scream, enough to shatter glass, as running juices leaked down her thighs. Her lips were on his. The taste of salt on his index finger, prominent in his mouth. Just another breath, not the release, and his hips collided with her own again. His hands lifted her hips up, gripping on as they both felt the build-up of climax.

"Claire…" The one single syllable was enough to stir her up.

Subsequently, she sat up in her bed. Sweat stuck to the sides of her face and there was shameful moisture elsewhere. It had confirmed on that Wednesday morning, at half past six, she had an aphrodisiac dream.

She sighed, flipping back the duvet cover as she clenched her eyes, feeling utterly ashamed of her lustful thoughts. It had her wondering if what Darren said was right and that she was horny bastard.

Why was she breathing so fast? God, she frowned, lifting her feet out of bed. How stupid. Claire shook her head, stood up, and headed for the bathroom. There was no point in even asking why. She knew why. And as for now, she had to focus on getting to work without dropping another lid shut and pondering on that erotic dream.

***

Zack must have been trying because on

Wednesday morning she was requested to return to the board in reconsideration of her position. As much as she wanted to boycott the establishment, she missed and needed her job. By the second hour, she was back at her desk, people whispering amongst themselves over her absence and Graves' suspicion following her like a hawk.

The board had apologised for their mistake, were told by request from the CEO that her position should be resumed and malicious attempts had been made to jeopardise her position, but nothing else was said as to who did it.

Claire felt some pity towards Zack, but then again, it was more than likely his fault for her job loss.

***

The coffee tasted horrid at work. It wasn't like the brand she liked; it was bland, and it made her mouth only drier. God, she hated Wednesdays. They were always in the middle of the week. Too close to Monday and too far from the weekend. Why couldn't it be Friday? She wanted to be at home, tucked up in her blue, soft blanket, eating an entire Galaxy bar whilst muttering to herself at criticising the film. Instead, she was here. At the table, adding another spoonful of coffee grains into her cup and sighing at the dreary scene of her colleagues tapping away at their keyboards.

Although it at least gave her some sense of normalcy, drew her mind into actual work than dwelling on Monday's catastrophe.

She wished Darren was here, but she knew that was selfish.

Perhaps that was her other concern for their relationship. Could they be open about it? It was bad enough last year when Claire was crowned employee of the year at the annual work party; she had covetous stares for several weeks. *Wouldn't they run wild if they were invited to this newfound information?*

But why was she even thinking like that? Claire did not normally care what others felt. After all, she had become a trendsetter in college when she turned up in her class with a giant penis drawn on her forehead. Long story, but it wasn't a sober night for her.

"God almighty," she grumbled to herself, flopping her head further onto her propped-up hand. Here she was again. Thinking about him. He who shall not be named kind of shit. Her job was supposed to keep her mind off things, but it just wasn't working. And what did she expect? His fucking name was plastered on the front of the building.

"You okay? I just wanted to say it's good to see you back. Graves announced to the department about what happened. I feel shitty about it…'cause at one point I thought you…*did.*" She looked up to see Jason settling himself into the chair opposite.

Claire felt defeated. It was like some member of the Ghostbusters had sucked her entire soul away into a vacuum. How she felt so lost, so indecisive, so empty. But she wasn't going to admit that to Jason. "It's fine. Hey, with evidence like they had, it would be pretty darn silly not to believe it. I'm just glad I'm back, too. You don't realise how much the day drags when you're sitting at home," she replied with a short sigh. "God." She pulled a face of grimace. "This coffee tastes horrid. They really need to up their game. I know this is snobbish, but I can taste its cheapness."

Jason laughed at that. "Hey, I agree. Although I'm more of a tea drinker, so I'm glad the teabags are at least decent here."

Claire nodded in agreement, smiling a little, genuinely thankful for some sort of communication with another.

Jason rubbed the bottom of his chin, flicking his eyes around the room as a pause filled the space in between before finally he plucked up a question. "So, where's Zack?"

"He's…away at the moment." It was the only response she could think of on the spot. What else could she have said except, *"Hey, did you know he's our boss?"* No, she just stuck with something that anyone could cook up as an excuse.

"Oh, not that—I was—" Jason blushed. Claire was unsure why, but before she managed a word, he continued hastily. "Graves was speaking about him earlier on the phone. Something about dismissal or something? I was just curious."

"Oh," Claire said. This was new to her. *So he had already left then?* What was his game plan next? "I don't actually know. He's not exactly staying at mine at the moment. He's…away, like I said."

"Ah, I see." Jason nodded, brushing his hands together awkwardly. "So, good weekend?"

Claire shrugged her shoulders. "Well, I suppose. It was my brother's wedding, so that was nice. Proud sisterly moment, you could call it. Other than that, it was all right. *You?* I saw your Facebook post. You booked a holiday?"

"Y-Yeah, I did. I booked some time off work. I thought I deserved some time to go backpacking in Europe. And…well, kinda because I met someone," Jason explained, itching his palm with his cheeks reddening slightly.

"Really? That's so good to hear—"

"It's not official…yet. We met online. She's from Germany…hence the Europe trip. I'm a little nervous to be honest," Jason interjected, a little distress in his tone.

"That is spontaneous, but I'm sure you'll be fine. She must mean something to you then. Love at first click?"

Jason cracked a nervous one. "Yeah, I suppose. I just wanted to do something. I know this isn't exactly good to bring up, but with Darren's…" He paused as he licked his bottom lip. "I just wanted to go for it. And—"

"I get it," Claire put in. "It's good. Do let me know how it goes."

"I will. So, how is Darren?"

Claire looked down into the fairly transparent liquid in her cup. "He's—he's all right. I mean, no. But he's coping. I think. Honestly, he…" She looked up at Jason. "He doesn't act the same. Like it literally is like a missing part of him has died along with his boyfriend. And I wish I could help him. But I can't."

"It sucks," Jason agreed solemnly. "Hey, tell him I send my love. You know? It is strange not having him around the office. After all, you could always hear Darren from where I sat."

"True." Claire smiled lightly. "And I will."

Jason nodded his head before he got up and headed out, returning to his desk that sat adjacent and little more than fifteen footsteps from the office's compact kitchen. Claire was grateful for that small interaction; it meant something. It fed her mind with healthy thoughts to take it all off Zack. And it was nice that things between them both weren't rocky considering a few months back, their friendship had become turmoil by the potential romance.

After three hours of tackling work, she headed to the sandwich bar down the road for lunch, tucking into two neatly cut triangles of tuna and sweetcorn. It was delicious, and it was able to fill that void in her stomach that had been attacking all morning. Guess she could say those cereal bars weren't exactly filling.

***

"God." Kyle coughed slightly, waving the smoke from his lips. "Try this. It's fucking weird but nice at the same time." He passed over a made-up cigarette towards Zack, who was preoccupied with the assortment of contracts that Olivia had kindly posted to him yesterday.

"Since when do you smoke?" Zack asked, receiving the cigarette. He was hesitant to take a puff as he frowned. "What is this, *anyway*? It smells like shit." Moving it in between his fingers, the retching smell licked the tips of his nostrils.

"Some herb. Oh, I don't know." Kyle smirked enthusiastically, clasping his hands together. "It's on trial. Some pal of mine recommended it. Just shove it in your mouth and *suck* on it."

Spurring Zack on, he slapped his friend's knee. Zack rolled his eyes, shoving the contracts on the coffee table before him away as he brought the cigarette to his lips. The taste was not so bad once it hugged his taste buds for a second or two. It didn't stop him from coughing, however.

"God…" He exhaled, passing the cigarette back. "That's some strong stuff."

"It's nice, though, right?" Kyle said before taking a long drag himself.

"It just fucking stinks."

"Just like weed then," Kyle replied, blissfully enjoying the taste upon his tongue. "So, anyway. How's all this going?" He dashed his hands towards the paperwork. "What are you actually thinking of doing?"

"Yeah, well, I am," Zack confirmed, suddenly distracted by his phone that he had swiped out from his back pocket. "Guess I'm just going to dance with fire. I have a plan to gain access to that money I spoke about that the business never sees. Get them to fund more of my projects. The one my father has control over. The chairman of board, I think, can be arguably persuaded if they are tempted by the flash of a little money here and there. My father gave them more control of it than me." He didn't remove his eyes from the screen.

"So, you're going to blackmail them?"

"Yeah, something like that..." Zack muttered, his brows scrunching together as he remained glued to his phone, ignorant to his friend's presence.

"Hey, what the fuck are you even looking at? You got some porn stashed on that thing?" Kyle blurted, snatching his phone from off him.

"Hey!" Zack exclaimed. "Not cool—"

"I thought you were giving the girl some time. Not messaging her. Jesus Christ, Zack, you were telling me earlier how you were going to give her time. And look here, you're already messaging her. God, you can't be obedient, can you?" Kyle interrupted, throwing his phone back into Zack's lap.

"Yeah, well. I can't help it. I guess you could say I'm not used to this—"

"Yeah, not used to not getting what you want," Kyle interjected, smirking as he took another drag from the cigarette.

"Fuck off, Kyle. I just...don't understand her. In fact, I don't understand women. First, they want us to come and console them, and then they're practically begging to be left alone. It makes no sense. And you know, I was pretty certain we would have come as close as having make-up sex on Monday. She jumped on me," Zack explained, vexed.

Kyle chuckled. "Just shut up about it and have another smoke of this. I don't feel like being your therapist today."

***

Claire's hand was already reaching for her mobile phone in her handbag. It had alerted her to a new message. She was not expecting it to be Zack.

Zack the Dick: So, hey.
Received 12:30pm

Claire's heart began to hammer against her ribcage. What was he doing? What did he even want? Had Monday not made her complete humiliation clear enough? She had also forgotten the nickname she had assigned to his contact. Here was another indication of how shit had gone to the fan.

Claire: What Zack?
Sent 12:32

Zack: How are you?
Received 12:32

Claire: Seriously? Zack, can we not?
Sent 12:33

Zack: Are we not going to talk about Monday?
Received 12:34

Claire sighed, turning away from her phone to look outside at the commotion of traffic caused by the road workers tarmacking the street. She needed something to take her mind off things, but how was that possible?

She felt the vibration of her phone in the palm of her hand, alerting her that Zack had messaged again.

She looked down towards the screen.

Zack: Claire? Are you there? Monday?
Received 12:37

Claire: No. I don't want to.
Sent 12:38

Zack: It must mean something, the kiss...I love you.
Received 12:38

She almost returned with, "I love you too," but she couldn't. Nor could she admit her reasons for that kiss. She just couldn't. Her mind was just clouded with negativity over this whole affair. She couldn't yet decide if it was a complete lie or a stubborn judgment on her behalf. And why? She didn't know, and that was what really ticked her off.

Zack: Claire.
Received 12:39

Claire: What?
Sent 12:39

Zack: We'll get through this, babe.
Received 12:40

Claire: I've got work. Bye, Zack.
Sent 12:41

Then she locked her phone, turning it onto silent and shoving it into her bag. Oh, how she felt like she was being the difficult one here and not the other way around.

CHAPTER THIRTEEN

ZACK

Not a word from Claire, and Zack was impressed by his own determination to remain silent. It had been exactly two days, which wasn't exactly a massive achievement, but it was already the weekend of the first week. In those two days, Zack was also able to blackmail the chairman of the board to allow him a subsidy from the stock of cash they were guarding. It worked like a charm. It went along the lines of almost mimicking a badass scene, Zack entering with a sword blazing with fire, its sharp, intimidating end threatening the greying elder closest to the door into cooperating. Then Zack summoned a lightning rod into the palm of his hand as he waved it about to grab the attention of the others to witness the signing of some contract that his assistant, Olivia, dressed in a black corset and rocking red and green hair, had pushed in front of the leading director. All the while, heavy metal blasted into the room with the chant of "sign it!" from several other wildly dressed employees he'd brought along to create the atmosphere of a gladiator arena. It left nothing but the shrivelled old men defenceless to agree and allow Zack to pursue his goal of turning the ship around.

Perhaps it didn't exactly go like that, but Zack was impressed by his complete, calm persuasiveness to encourage the stuck-up, stubborn men to change their minds. It just required the ingredient of money to get things cooking. It went more a little along the lines of this:

"Good afternoon, gentlemen," Zack announced as the wooden doors swung open into the conference room. The six men sat around a round table like King Arthur and his Knights. With grace, Zack slid a black briefcase onto the head of the table, startling the men further, who were already blinking and scratching their chins. "Great weather, isn't it? Hope I'm not interrupting." He composed himself, hoping that it was enough to acknowledge his power within these premises. "Now, I won't keep you long, as I know you have plenty of work to do for my father, who..." Zack paused deliberately, scanning around the room. "...is nowhere to be seen.

Perhaps he retired?" His sarcasm made a few red faces amongst the group. "Anyway, how's this work for you?" Snapping his fingers gently, he instructed Olivia to open the briefcase.

Inside was more than enough to make a grown man cry with joy. Money. Lots and lots of it. "Nice, isn't it, fellas?" Zack interjected, cocking his right eyebrow up. "Now, I'm sure we wouldn't mind coming to an agreement over my access towards that hefty lot of money. Now what would we say if…" He clicked his tongue upon the roof of his mouth. "If this money somehow increased your wages?"

There was not a sound in the room. The men remained dumbfounded, but through Zack's eyes, he could see them clocking it up in their minds. "Now, all you fellas have to do is direct the money elsewhere. Say, a new project that I am already running."

Now, it was their turn to answer.

The one sat in the centre glanced towards the other slightly greying elder, whose plump face, sunken blue eyes, and rounding belly indicated for sure that this was a man entitled to greed.

There was a short conversation between the two before finally the one spoke. "I think…" He paused as he licked his bottom lip, the greying moustache above his lip kissed with sweat. "I think we could come to a compromise, Mr. Benson. We could have that money immediately transferred towards your project."

He swallowed as he sat a little back.

"Great." Zack smiled, snapping shut the briefcase. "I'll have significant rises put towards your wages. Pleasure doing business with you," he said, lifting the case up as he began to head towards the doors, Olivia meekly following after him. "Oh, and one other thing…" Zack stopped short, his frustration disguised by his growing smile. "Come short of your end of the deal and I'll have each one of you fired and served with a miserable lawsuit. Guess your histories don't add up well for you fellas. Wasn't one of you suspected of supplying illegal drugs to gangs? Or did I get the wrong end of the stick?" He grew more confident by the second due to the sudden distress of one of the men, whose face flushed red. "Have a nice afternoon, fellas." Zack held the door open as he summoned Olivia to pass by him, allowing him a final lingering expression of satisfaction.

Closing the door behind him, he thanked Olivia for her supply of information on all six men as they headed down the corridor. It would have been a lot more pleasing to just dismiss them all, but infinitely they were blessed by their experience and running of the entire business for him to dispose of them. So they had to stay. It didn't mean he couldn't swap them around and make a more cooperative board in time, but for now they remained under his wing, tempted by the wag of a bone. His father said not to play with fire…but Zack was disobedient when it came to rules.

***

CLAIRE

Claire was fed up. Of course, she didn't need to worry about the rent as Zack had already paid for his half and "kindly" but without her consent paid for another month's rent. That again made her feel more like the bad guy.

It also sucked living alone in the apartment. It felt different than when she was alone after Abbey left to reside with her boyfriend. At least then she could cope…now, it just felt so lonely, and without the petty arguments, the wild sex, and the enjoyment of having Zack around, she now hated coming back home to her empty apartment. She didn't get to have somebody embrace her at night, tell her the food sucked when she attempted a new recipe, or listen to his irritating moaning about hoovering. There was no need for rules or regulations over leaving the toilet seat up, putting dirty laundry in the basket, or picking up food crumbs. None of that. It felt weird to be given back her independence.

Surely, she shouldn't have minded? But she

did. She missed him. What else did she expect? Of course, she still loved him. Her judgment was just overruled by his lies. Did she actually know him? Was he still the same man? Zack Benson…was he really the Zack Chase she had grown to love? It sounded like she was trying to say that there was more than one. That Zack Chase had somehow been kidnapped and replaced with Benson. That was obtuse. Zack had to still be Zack. Right?

As for work, one thing had drastically happened. And no, that wasn't Claire's long campaign to get an upgrade for better coffee beans was accepted. It was that Monica no longer worked for Benson's Corporation. While she would have loved to have seen the woman leave because of dismissal, she was in fact leaving on her own grounds. It came as such a surprise, but not really a surprise for why.

Monica, who had been Claire's and Darren's thorn in their sides for the past four years, was leaving. It was on Thursday morning when she announced her decision, her faded red curls clipped to the side and a tissue in her hand. Graves was standing nearby, a little distant towards the commotion but nonetheless present. It looked as if she were about to cry, but if there was one thing Claire knew, it was that Monica was able to put on a show.

Clutching her tissue and ensuring it was the hand where her large engagement ring could be on show, she said in a weak, most award-winning performance of sounding distressed that she was leaving. "My fellow colleagues," she had begun, causing Claire to roll her eyes. What was this, a beauty pageant? "I'm calling quits today, for I am leaving…" She paused once again to add dramatic effect.

"To head off to Milan with my fiancé." There were a few gasps in the audience, perhaps those who had literally worshipped Monica. But if not, many were just content like Claire to be given some time off from working to listen to this woman speak. "We are building a fashion business together!" she exclaimed excitedly, changing her tune suddenly from that dismal state to a woman who looked as if she won the lottery.

"However," she added, lifting her index finger up, her red lips smiling haughtily, "I couldn't leave without you guys meeting my groom-to-be." Then she happily jumped on her toes, beckoning a man to come out who was hiding inside Graves' office.

Claire's mouth snapped open like an alligator. Was she surprised? Yes and no. An aging, greying man dressed in yellow chinos, a white polo top, and several golden rings on his fingers with black sunglasses covering his eyes appeared from the office. It had to be a joke, but it clearly wasn't when he hobbled on over, sliding his hand around her waist.

Claire could see some expressions of humour on several of her colleagues' faces, but most just consisted of pure shock.

"What on earth?" she heard a few mutters. Much to the male population's disappointment, the woman they had slept around with had found an old man, old enough to be her grandfather, digging his dick in for gold.

Bon voyage to that cow at least.

"Oh, I'm gonna miss you guys so much." She gave a fake display of affection as she cuddled some at the front at arm's length whilst her aging fiancé looked deliciously content.

Claire also noticed how Graves was itching with jealousy and appeared ticked off by this news. As if he hadn't heard it already from Monica, he had to watch as she publicly announced her departure and give not a lick of affection towards her old lover.

"Farewell, children." Claire could hear Monica's patronising tone follow her into the kitchen even as she shut the door to block out the sound. She couldn't stand that woman.

At least it was great news to share with Darren, who she had almost forgot was not standing there with her and was instead at home. Sliding her phone open, she disregarded the unopened email notifications and phoned Darren up.

"Hello, Darren?" Claire said, a little too urgently down the phone.

"Yeah, what's up? I'm here," he replied and heard the shutdown of voices in the background what she suspected was the television he had become so accustomed to each and every day.

"I have some good news. And boy, do you wish you were—I mean—" Claire stopped short as she flushed red, knowing that Darren was still in too much distress to be thinking of attending work nor worrying himself over good office gossip. "Erh—"

"Spit it out, woman." Darren chuckled a little, surprising Claire by his encouragement. "What news?" It was almost there for a second, he sounded like his old self.

"Monica is leaving," Claire said nonchalantly.

"Oh my god! Really?"

"Yes. And she's marrying some old guy, and they're heading off to Milan."

Darren exhaled down the line. "Boy, our Monica, a gold digger. Not surprised, but..." He paused for a second. "I'm actually going to miss the bitch. Never thought I'd say that, but we've had our fun with our bitching sessions over that woman. Now, she's heading off. Good riddance, but damn, how...things just change like that," he muttered, confirming to Claire that he was in deep thought. Still not the same old Darren that she knew.

Keeping the same casual tone as her friend, she agreed. "Yeah, off she goes. To make a fashion business, as she has kindly shared. Graves doesn't look too pleased. Confirms he was enjoying their affair even if she clearly wasn't into him, however he saw things. But yeah, no more Monica."

"Gives your boyfriend one less job to think about—oh, wait," Darren apologised. "Zack—"

"No, it's...fine," Claire reassured herself, nodding as she twirled her index finger upon the table. "I'm starting to reconsider things these past two days. I'm slowly getting there." She wondered if that meant she was able to push aside all this and start things all over again.

"You'll get there. Just keep thinking it over, babe."

Claire exhaled. "Yeah...so, how are you today?"

Darren yawned. "Well...I'm just watching some Jeremy Kyle at the moment. I have some other stuff I've got to attend to later..." The lingering silence afterwards made her very suspicious, yet only for that second. "And then, nothing. You're welcome to come around after work. I could do with the company, and well, I'm sure being alone in that apartment isn't exactly healthy towards your judgment on things," he offered.

"Yeah, that would be great," Claire replied, smiling slightly to herself. "Hey, I'll let you get on. I better get back before my presence is missed, and I wouldn't want to miss Monica standing there, holding a bunch of flowers as if she had won the goddamn Miss World Competition."

Darren laughed a little at that, but it was too soon before his weak, defeated voice returned. "Yeah, I'll see you later, Claire."

With another round of goodbye, Claire ended the call and slipped her phone back into her suit trousers' pocket. It wasn't any revelation that, as she exited the kitchen, Monica was still being pampered by those who adored her. It made no sense. Those people must be on drugs to think that woman was a kind, considerate, and fair woman.

Claire had expected to hobble back over to her desk with no interference, but Graves appeared, startling her as he tapped on her shoulder. "Can we talk please?" He pointed his finger towards the office door as he barely made eye contact. His attention was still diverted by his old lover, who was laughing and moving her body closer towards her older man. Her hands remained around the old's man neck as he shoved an unlit brown cigar in his mouth.

As Claire passed them, Graves warned for the man not to smoke, shunning his eyes away from Monica. This time she stopped short to glance at the man she had fooled into thinking she loved him. What a fucked-up love story, Claire thought, entering the office and listening as the door shut after them.

"Monica no longer holds her position," Graves said, gesturing his hand towards a chair so Claire could sit down. "I think I can now reconsider that placement." Walking behind Claire, he suddenly placed a hand on her shoulder. She refrained herself from jumping up, not knowing what the gesture was suggesting, nor did she want to take it the wrong way around. Yet thankfully, its position there was brief. He was not attempting to suggest anything inappropriate.

Graves walked around his desk, not taking a seat, but standing behind his chair. "The promotion is there for you, Miss Winter. Do you accept?" he asked solemnly.

This incompetent, selfish man was now providing her the one thing she had wanted since last year. That one fucking promotion she'd thought she had in her reach until Monica got the position. And had things changed around here? No. She had the chance now. The chance to make things right. The position offered more money, more packages into her pension, holidays, and more influence within the department. It was right there in front of her. Right in her hands.

"So? You can start immediately, right now. What is your answer, Claire?" Graves asked once again.

She was literally a word away.

"No."

Gone. That was it. She had said it.

"No?" Graves reiterated with an expression of confusion. "Surely, this is what you've worked for, Claire. Are you certain?"

"No." She nodded. "I have to say no, Mr. Graves. I cannot take the placement. I'm sorry, but I do not want it." And with that as her final answer towards his proposition, she stood up, thanked him for the offer, and left without his consent. She wasn't going to accept a job that she knew was hers from the beginning, a job that had been tainted by the likes of Monica because Graves couldn't keep his stiff member from jumping into action. Her hard work was not going to be subjected to that just because the man was suddenly angered by Monica's departure.

And why was she not surprised that just as Monica was about to leave, Graves announced that Susan—the office's one and only gossiper—was appointed as his second in command. That same job he had offered Claire only moments ago. That was why. It wasn't done out of consideration, only as pure mockery towards Monica, who gaped a little from his quick action at replacing her only an hour later. And besides, she couldn't work under a man who treated his colleagues how he has, and what's saying she would even manage a word in?

***

At the end of her shift, Claire was exhausted. She still had to go back into the building to retrieve her bag and head off home, but as for now, she was content with just lingering outside the fire exit door, taking in some air.

She didn't want to move; she just wanted to stand there at the back of the building where she was, looking up at the sky.

From the corner of her eye, she saw a car suddenly pull up; a fairly middle-aged man opened the back door before returning to the driver's seat. Out of curiosity, she remained where she was, her hand resting on the handle as she saw another fire exit door open down at the bottom of the building to where she believed whoever was being escorted out of the building to the car would exit.

Claire almost fell to her knees at the sight of Zack, holding his phone to his ear as he passed through the door. She had thought the distraction of his phone was enough to keep him on target, but a swift look towards the left brought him to meet her gaze.

She held her breath. She couldn't look away, nor did she want to. How badly she wanted to run up to him and throw her arms around his neck, but her feet argued otherwise, remaining in her place. She had expected Zack to drop everything and flee over, but instead, he moved the phone slowly towards his chest and just smiled. It was that type of smile that was sympathetic or trying to offer a route of ease. It was weak. Barely evoking the same energy as a full spread one.

It pained her. She could see how he was trying to restrain himself. It lasted only for a second longer before he lifted the phone back to his ear and got into the car. The door shut, and the car drove on.

Time she asked of him, and time he was giving her. But why was she so unsure now?

CHAPTER FOURTEEN

ZACK

The car was too far in steady, fast acceleration for Zack to abruptly change his mind and run back after Claire. There was the option of jumping out the car, rolling onto the side of road, hoping it was possible to dodge a few cars before landing onto his two feet like he was James Bond escaping from danger. Yet he wasn't exactly trained as a stuntman in a movie, nor was he an agent enlisted with the task of saving the world. So staying in that comfortable, black leather seat seemed more appropriate. Besides, he was attempting to stay at a distance from Claire, despite the nagging thought of wanting to do opposite.

Zack slid open the lock screen on his phone, his fingers hovering over her name. Maybe he could just call her? See how she was or explain why he hadn't come over, just in case she hadn't put two and two together? But he didn't press the button; instead, he very much sighed with exasperation and shoved his phone back into his navy blue blazer's pocket.

Glancing up to look ahead onto the road, he took notice as Wickes missed the turn to his usual route home. "Er, you *missed* the turn, Wickes." He chuckled, his index finger following the passing scenery adjacent to him.

"Sorry, sir. It was deliberate. Your mother has requested your presence," he replied in his usual reserved and composed tone. Wickes turned right, accelerating as he hit a forty zone, then flicked his eyes towards the rear mirror as he saw the growing vexation upon Zack's face. "I believe it is another house gathering."

"Well, isn't that *great*," Zack grumbled, sitting back as he began to adjust his watch. "Just what I wanted."

Wickes offered an understanding smile. "I believe she *strictly* instructed me to ensure your arrival. No *other* options were given." In the back, Zack gave a weak smirk, shaking his head as he knew all too well there was no saying no to that woman. "Well," Zack inhaled, glancing out the window as they crossed into the country lanes. "Let's *not* anger the queen."

His parents' residence soon came into view, the twisting green vines running up at the side trellis extending up the sides of the manor. The usual stone columns forming the structure of the front stood proud and polished, and already he could see hired valets collecting guests' cars as they headed inside. Zack cringed. He despised these sorts of parties, particularly ones that involved his parents' guests, who were outright stuck up and couldn't tell you the meaning of walking. Oh no, you had to be served as if you were a baby unable to move and twitch a finger.

"Shall I wait for you?" Wickes asked, parking the car near the edge of the lawn.

"Yes, I'm hoping I won't be here for long. Otherwise, please just do come in and enjoy yourself, Wickes. Take a glass of champagne, maybe *two*, *three,* or *four*. There's got to be a fucking dozen in here," Zack replied as he exited the car.

Wickes chuckled before pulling out his phone, causing Zack to smile. If he knew that man, then he knew he would exactly be tapping his finger towards catch-up TV and comfortably sitting there for however long he had to, enjoying a couple soaps. Zack shut the door, his feet crunching against the gravel as he sighed once more at the sight of some late arrivals heading indoors. Just what he needed.

There was the struggle at these sort of parties, complete concentration for one, could just easily slip at the sound of a monotonous tone dragging on as one bragged about their achievements or discussed business. The majority of the females here dressed extravagantly and laughing tirelessly at another's joke were housewives. And of course, they were tied up with drama; it came with the package of marrying one of these women. A rumour here and there and that summed up their tedious lives. Zack had heard a few; he could remember at his last attendance one woman had spread that another was flirting with the pool boy who was half her age whilst the husband dallied with a secretary at work. Just how cliché! No, when you walked through these parties, you could see nothing but falsities. You could see the insecurities of those who mistrusted their husbands, the odd gold digger scattered about, and the growing smiles on their faces. A true reflection in the mirror.

Take for instance now Zack, as he meandered through the grand living room, saw a wandering but not lost husband was flirting shamefully with another woman he was not wed to. Typical. Although this was not the case for everyone. As for Zack's parents' marriage, that was genuine, and the few elderly couples standing by appeared true enough.

But dear mercy did Zack hate these parties. If it wasn't enough to reply with hello here and there to whoever glanced his way, it was refraining from collecting more than one glass from the hired waiter's board.

The food selection was all right, partly

because the small cakes were delicious. The food was small, meant to be nibble size, no choice to choose something sloppy or sticky; it would be a disgrace to offer a guest dolled up in a gown or suit something messy. And as for the music, he could already see a hired pianist in the far corner of the dining room. No CD playing from a stereo was allowed. It was all about keeping up appearances with these sorts of parties. Even as a child, Zack could not be allowed to run or play but stand at the foot of his parents and brother as they spoke and only answer when spoken to. Manners, manners, and manners was the word drummed into him as a child, not that he couldn't see the good in them, but at parties, it was different. His plum cheeks had been squeezed so many times by strangers as a child that he was sure he'd be stuck with permanent marks. He hated cooing; it was as if he were a toy or diamond necklace on display.

There, standing in a blue gown, embroidered in diamonds across the waist and her hair stuck up in a fancy do, was his mother, laughing as another woman across from her spoke with a glass of champagne or perhaps prosecco within her hand.

"Mother," Zack said, interrupting whatever conversation she was engaged with. Turning her attention immediately towards her son, she blinked several times, a notion he knew flashed her vexation. "Can I *please* speak to you for a moment?" Ignoring her displeasure, he gestured towards the door adjacent to the grand bookcase of pointless books he knew neither of his parents had read; it was only to give the appearance of being studious.

"Sure, *Zack*." She smiled, evidently ticked off yet not wanting to appear to be so in front of guests. "Please excuse me, Sandra. I must go *speak* with my son. Enjoy the party, please do."

Following after Zack, they headed into the study, a room that was very familiar to Zack for its ebony woodwork, dark green curtains, and occasionally lit fireplace. Even looking towards the bar, Zack could remember of the many times he saw his father sitting in the armchair as a young teenager, listening to his father speak of the business and how one day it would be either himself or Jared enlisted with such a great task.

"How dare you interrupt me like that, Zack?" his mother spat, releasing a handful of her gown she had held to prevent her from tripping up. "I was speaking, and you know how I hate it when people butt in. Whatever did I teach you, Zack? Where are your good manners?" Shaking her head, she frowned towards her son, who was taking not the slightest notice.

"Mom, what is this? Do I seriously have to be here? You know I hate keeping up my appearances," Zack pointed out, dismissing her disgust.

"Yes, and that is precisely the reason I invited you over. So do not think for one second you are leaving. Jared is here too, somewhere. I'd like it if you polish up this attitude and make yourself useful by attending to guests out there. You know this is important for you in finding more investors and for getting your name out there."

Zack sighed. "Fine."

"Oh, and now that you're finally here, you can meet someone," his mother piped up, clasping her hands together. "Follow me. You're not getting yourself out of this one, young man." She picked up her dress as she headed back towards the door and ushered Zack to keep up. He knew this meant meeting a candidate for his possible partner in marriage. Despite telling his mother countless times before to remain distant from that part of his life, he knew that wouldn't stop her.

Zack had to look a little pleased to be here as they meandered back through the crowd of people, replying with a hello here and there and smiling when he needed to. God, he hated parties.

"Zack, I'd like you to meet Angela Stockson," his mother introduced, pointing indirectly towards the woman before him, who oddly was not who he had expected. In some sense, he had expected her to have a polished look and at least look rather stuck up, but instead, her blonde hair was left in its natural beach waves, accented with blue dyed tips. Several piercings covered her face, two on her bottom lip and a septum through her nose. There was no full coverage makeup, and her choice of gown was simple and effective, taking the competition away from all the other neighbouring females. All in all, she was a very beautiful woman, but just not enough to set his heart racing like someone he knew. "I will leave you two to it."

"Hey there, handsome." She jutted her chin out.

Zack smirked, immediately liking her confidence. "Hey, yourself."

"Let's go outside," she perkily declared, pushing her hair to one side. "Keep up, handsome." Turning on her heel, she began to weave through the guests, barely taking notice of those who looked at her in disgrace over her poor posture and frantic rush. Without breathing a word back, Zack followed in pursuit, her chocolate brown dress in sight as they headed out into the garden.

Once there, she shuffled over to one of the marble stone benches, taking a seat before digging her hand down her chest to retrieve a packet of cigarettes. Zack wasn't sure if he shouldn't have looked, but she seemed confident enough to not even care if he had. Slipping the roll-up between her lips, she held it there as she took out a lighter to ignite the tobacco he could see she craved. A little hesitant at first, Zack finally sat down next to her, resting his elbows onto his knees as his eyes stayed glued to the ground.

"Mmmm, god, I needed that," she exhaled, a puff of smoke dancing away from her lips. "Want one?"

"I'm good." Zack nodded, declining her offer as he sat a bit more back and began to roll back his sleeves.

"So…" Exhaling out again. "You want to fuck upstairs?"

Zack coughed, hitting his chest several times. "*Whoa*, you're quick. I mean—any other day I would have, but—" His laughter died a little as he began to run a hair through his thick, jet black hair.

She chuckled before taking another quick drag. "I get it." She paused for a second as she flicked some of the dried tobacco at the end. "That is the sound of someone who is smitten and head over heels in love. Although I'm little surprised you don't remember me."

"I—wait, we've *met* before?" Zack frowned a little, trying hard to pick up any memory from the scrutiny of her facial features.

Angela hooted with laughter. "Man, you were really being a fuckboy. Baby, I'm a *little* offended that you forget this face going down on you." Zack consciously glanced down to his trousers. "It's fine, though," she continued, taking another short puff. "I didn't think you would. I sorta changed appearance." She smiled towards him. "But still nothing?" She shook her head with disbelief as Zack shook his head.

"*Okay.*" She sighed a little. "Picture me with a simplistic, bitch look. Y'know, blonde curled waves, no piercings, supposedly an innocent woman and barely any boobs." Then she hissed in a whisper, "I had a boob job." She pulled a shocked, dramatic face, causing Zack to smile with amusement.

"Anyway, I altered one day. I just thought, fuck it. I'm sick of people judging me. Seeing me as little Miss Stockson, daughter of Wayne and Daphne Stockson. *Little Miss Perfect.* So I cut my hair but…" She paused, tugging a strand of her hair and shaking it about. "It's grown since then." She dropped it back into place. "Got piercings, several tattoos that would you believe are all under this gown and totally pissed off my parents."

"Wow," Zack said, raising his brows. "Fair play."

"I know, right?" She smiled, exhaling as she stretched her arms out and flicked the cigarette onto the floor before digging her heel onto it. "So I kinda suspected you wouldn't remember me. After all, when we fucked, I was *daddy's little princess.*"

Zack nodded his head, acknowledging to

himself that he must have slept with this attractive woman. Not that he was surprised…back then he'd slept around. "So when…did we fuck?" he asked with curiosity, watching as her face lit up with amusement.

"Oh, sometime last year. It was at your friend's party. Kyle, right?"

"Yeah."

"Well, we hooked up in the guest bedroom. You had me all over. Rear, front, side to side," she blabbered on, deliberately counting on her fingers as she held onto that growing mischievous smile. "Fuck, you even had me bending over onto that expensive table that you took the piss out of earlier when Kyle beckoned for no one to touch it."

Zack nodded his head several times. "Well, that must have been nice."

Angela laughed, shoving his shoulder. "Man, fuckboy, all over."

"Yeah."

"So who's the lucky one?"

Zack swallowed. "The lucky one?"

"Y'know, this woman who's stopping you from taking me upstairs, Mister," she said, leaning back on her elbows as she slid her bottom onto the ground.

Zack kissed his teeth. "I don't know what you're talking about."

"Okay, *okay*," Angela repeated, surrendering her hands into the air. "Tell me otherwise, I'll *won't* stop for a second to pull down those trousers and suck on that—"

"Okay, damn, you're horny as fuck," Zack interjected, grinning from ear to ear. She really was a fun person, just not who he was thinking of getting down to their knees and pleasuring the fuck out of him. "It's complicated."

"Complicated?"

"Yeah, complicated."

Angela groaned. "What? You messing about with a married woman? Some—"

"No, I fucked up. But I just can't understand why me refusing to back down and not doing the usual dick move and leaving a woman to mope, she keeps pushing me away and wants time. Like, I don't understand you women. You complain when you want the man, but when he tries, you push him away," Zack explained, not even caring that as he slipped down onto his bum to join her on the ground, there were a few lingering stares coming from indoors through the glass.

"Let 'em stare," she hissed, smiling as she took notice. Then she inhaled, turning back towards Zack. "I believe I can't help you on that because I can be the same. I suppose that's makes us so damn lovable. You really love her?"

"Yeah."

Angela hummed to herself, a gesture of amusement. "Well, then, don't listen. I mean, she's gotta like you for being so determined. I mean, I know I would. Just balance it out."

"Well, gee, thanks," Zack replied, moaning as he dropped his head back to look at the sky. "And just so you know, Miss Angela, this look suits you better."

"Well, thanks, handsome." She laughed in return, following with the same motion to shift her eyes up to the sky. "And just so you know, the loved-up puppy eyes suit you. Do you mind if I have it with your brother?"

"Be my guest."

Leaving Angela, he tried to look like he was pleasing his mother's wishes, he mingled about with other guests, ignoring the fact he could see his father across the other side of the room, casually looking over with an amusing smile plastered on his face.

It was only a short while after he'd complimented some woman's attire, making her blush like a beetroot, that his father stumbled over, plopping a glass of whisky in his hand as he tagged Zack along with his stroll.

"*Dad*," Zack calmly said, smiling on the outside as he continued to parade that perfection towards guests.

"*Zack*," his father replied, jerking his glass up to one of the elderly men who waved towards Elijah.

"What interests you this time?" Zack asked as they headed into a quieter space. It was a struggle to keep his smile projecting through his gritted teeth.

"A little birdie told me you'd persuaded the board into funding some unknown project. I hope you're not planning on anything, Zack. I'd—*oh*, hello, Davis." His father abruptly halted his words, cheerfully addressing the man who'd entered along with his wife through the front doors, dressed from head to toe in pink feathers; surely, you'd think they got hitched in Vegas. "Please, go ahead. Spirits up ahead, champagne for the lady," he added, gesturing his free hand to the side of him before he continued in that hoarse, deadly tone. "I told you to stick to the correct path, didn't I?"

"Why, yes." Zack smiled, slapping his hand on his father's back as a photographer passed by and snapped a photo. "Just doing you proud!" he said aloud, enticing his father to join in his false show of laughter.

"That's my boy!"

Elijah stopped Zack in his tracks. "If I find out you're messing around with those stupid ideas of yours, I'll step in Zack."

"Haven't you already been?" Zack spat slyly before drifting off in the other direction.

***

At least, for the remainder of the time he

spent at the party, he had Angela to talk to. It was better than conversing with those who were too busy parading around their perfect lives. At around eight o'clock, he left, got in the car, and Wickes drove him home after he'd found him snoring his head off as his phone on his lap, continuing to play a soap he had been watching before he fell asleep.

Zack was exhausted; he just didn't have the energy in him to make it upstairs to his bedroom. Loosening his tie off and kicking off his shoes, he fell flat onto the sofa, grabbing the nearest pillow as he relaxed his head on it comfortably.

It must have literally only been a second when he heard his front door. Annoyed, he shouted out, "Door!" He realised soon after he'd sent the maid off on a week's holiday, meaning there was only him left in that lonely, complex penthouse.

There was another series of knocks. "Okay, okay, I'm coming!" he bellowed, nearly slipping on the floor as he attempted to find his balance. With more struggles, he finally got up and hobbled over as he rubbed his eyes.

A yawn locked onto him that as he opened the door. It almost immediately dispersed away at the sight of his unexpected guest. "Claire?" Blinking several times at the brunette standing there, her hair tied up in some messy bun, and today's clothes wrinkled by the looks of a few hours' nap.

"Hi," she muttered, this time her eyes anxiously stuck onto his. "Can I come in?"

"Sure—yeah, come in." He moved aside as his heart began to thunder as she entered and stood patiently only a few steps forward. Her eyes looked around in awe, intimidated by how huge the place was. If it wasn't for the fact that nearly all the lights were off, she probably would have continued to look around. "Sorry, I just got back," Zack excused himself, heading for the light switch until she protested.

"No, keep them off. It's nice seeing the skyline." She gestured towards the huge glass windows staring out onto the city.

"Sure," he said, walking back over and not knowing what else to do except shove his hands down his pockets. "Di—"

"So—"

"Sorry." Zack chuckled, his eyes lingering on her blushing cheeks at their unexpected clash of words. *"You first."*

Claire smiled weakly as she walked down to the sofa. "So what did you come from?"

"A party—parents' party. It was shit, like normal," he replied, moving to just beside her. "Should have seen all the snobs there. It's pathetic how all those people try to mirror the perfect lives."

Claire chuckled a little. "I suppose I wouldn't fit in then. Having to laugh when something isn't funny or look at least like royalty."

"You would fit in," Zack muttered. "I mean, I'd have to teach you, you know, the tricks of the trade for dealing with these people, but I would just teach you to be you. 'Cause you're perfect."

He offered a smile that she couldn't see as her back still faced him. She had found his note then. The address he left for her to find just in case she changed her mind or ever needed to speak to him. And she would have found the stack of cash he left for the month's rent.

"Zack," she breathed.

"Yeah?"

She turned. "I shouldn't be here. This—"

"Wait, don't go," Zack begged, gently touching the air that was inches away from her arm. "You must have come for a reason, Claire."

"I don't know," she confessed, tears threatening to fall. "I honestly don't know."

Zack didn't want to push her away. He couldn't force her nor intrude on her feelings. She was still vulnerable, still struggling by the lie he'd dealt. But all cards were on the table now. No more secrets. "Well, just come sit down. We can watch a movie. I hardly use that box." He pointed towards the television stand. "Or we could…sit and talk…doesn't have to be about us. It could be about anything. Just—" He paused, raking his hand through his hair. "Just come sit down. I promise that's all."

"Pinky promise?" Zack tested, lifting his little finger up.

A smile flourished onto her lips, only just about, however. "O-okay."

Zack sighed inside with relief, dropping his hand as he scooted towards the television and turned it on. Claire stood where she was, unsure what to do until finally her feet managed to move into motion. She dropped down onto the sofa, placing her hands in her lap as she looked outside.

"Ah, dang it," she heard him grumble. "Fucking Kyle has broken my TV. Pardon my French." He pulled back and rested his hands onto his hips. "Er, so no movie. But—"

"Are you sure it's broken?" she interjected, gently getting up to her feet. Zack nodded, gesturing his hand towards the television. Cautious not to stand too close to him, she glanced at the TV before scooting around the back, thankful she could still see by the intruding light from the city behind her. She smirked at its culprit.

"What's *that* smile for?" Zack asked, loving and shamefully aware that it was turning him on.

"It's broken, is it?" She lifted up the plug that was resting on the floor behind the TV.

Zack was lost for words. "Well, I guess—"

"Plug it in next time, dummy." She laughed

lightly, plugging it into the socket.

"I knew that." Zack coughed to clear his throat as he scratched his chin.

No wonder he loved this girl.

Claire tucked back a strand of hair as she hesitated whether to return to the sofa or remain where she stood.

She was doomed. The man she had been trying to stay away from was merely an arm's length away and was no figment of her imagination. His tousled black forest of hair was clear as day, those broad shoulders clung close to his white linen shirt, and those round kissable lips moved as he spoke.

Her fingers grazed against the surface of one of the painted golden buttons attached to her black peacoat, its purpose to fight against the slightly chilly autumn temperatures. It was unable to fight against the growing goose bumps crawling across her arms that surfaced because of Zack. Anxiously, her fingers continued to move, pausing before they tugged on the ends of her red scarf.

"And we have lift off," Zack commented as the television screen flooded with life. "I guess next time I should *remember* to see if the damn thing is plugged in." He gave slight, apprehensive chortle. Claire said nothing and only continued itching her nails against the soft red cotton as Zack headed for the sofa and sat down.

In the background, the audible sound of two TV presenters discussing the latest news distracted Claire's attention for a second. All in all, she knew she was fucked. She knew coming here was a huge mistake, but she couldn't deny the invisible cord pulling her to him. Perhaps it was because of today, seeing him, that vulnerability painted on his face, or it was just because she couldn't bear to leave him alone.

Zack flicked on Netflix, quickly scanning through the movies as they popped up on the screen. "So there's…some chick flicks, horror…erm…" He paused as he clicked his tongue upon the root of his mouth. "We could watch—"

"Zack," she interrupted, surprised by her intervention as his eyes suddenly pinpointed onto her. She took notice of the lines surrounding the base of his eyes; it appeared he must have been getting no sleep.

"Yeah?"

***

CLAIRE

From the little time she had been within his penthouse, Claire had grown more at a loss. Each corner of the place was materialistic: grand kitchen behind her, large towering bookcases situated in what appeared to be the dining room to the left of her, and decorative ornaments all around the place that looked as if they been imported from continents all around the world. None of it fitted with her superstore décor.

That was one of her other problems with the situation. How on earth were they going to make it work? Realistically, they were polar opposites on a scale, he rich and she an average worker. What could she expect but her independence slowly melting away? Would she even be expected to work anymore? Would he expect that of her? Those were some of the questions she was asking herself.

And who would accept that they helplessly had fallen in love without accusations flying about of her just digging for money? Heck, yeah, Claire had been able to dismiss what people thought about her as a young adult, but this was a major thing. This wasn't like that one college year when a few bitchy girls started a few rumours about her. No, this was different. Claire would care what people thought of her. It would diminish her confidence, make her more insecure, and slowly she would see herself falling out of character. She didn't want to lose herself. Not her energy. So how was their romance going to work? And the lying? She knew little of Zack, really. She didn't know who he really was. He could just be a really good liar for all she could tell. None of it was fitting well.

So what was she going to say? Do? Why was she even here?

And another thing: why was she so stubborn?

But she didn't speak. She didn't say a word. She'd given up. Claire knew what she was doing, knew it was sly, but she couldn't stop herself. She grasped the remote control out of his hand and switched off the television, ignoring the fact they'd spent a little more than five minutes attempting to get the thing to work in the first place.

Placing it gently back onto the coffee table, she swept in front of him, slowly taking off her coat before removing her scarf, then putting both garments at Zack's side, carefully. All this while, Zack did not utter a word.

"*Please.*" She clasped both his hands as she held them apart. Claire stooped down as she slid down onto his lap and rested her hands on his shoulders. "Kiss me," she whispered, running her right hand around the back of his neck. Then she leaned in, pressing her lips to his ear as she purred, "Fuck me, Zack." Shivers shot down the back of his spine.

He could feel his tongue drying with thirst and his friend below hardening, yet he was still baffled by her behaviour. It just didn't feel right. "*Claire,*" he said, frowning slightly, distracted by how her body was grinding against him as she squeezed her hands onto his biceps. "Claire, you're *not* thinking straight." He bit his tongue at the striking sensation washing over him. She didn't stop however and only continued to tempt him more, her teeth playing with the lobe of his ear as she rubbed her breasts against his chest.

"*Please*," she said softly, indulging him further into her desire as she slipped her right hand into his trousers, deliberately stroking his dick that was trapped by the black cotton of his boxer briefs. "Zack, I'm here. I want you to." She pecked the corner of his lips.

It just didn't make sense to him. It didn't feel like Claire. Something was telling him that she wasn't thinking it through, but it couldn't overthrow the driving power of lust that he had for the woman. Heck, how could he resist the way her body was pushing against his or that sensual, soft groan he'd swore he heard leave her lips at feeling him whilst he sat there, itching with impulse?

"Clai—"

He couldn't finish his sentence as she slammed her lips against his, shoving her tongue into his mouth as she wrapped her arms tightly around his neck. He didn't know how first to respond, whether this was some sort of test or if he had completely just imagined all of this, but she was reluctant to let go, and so he echoed her drive back. Fisting his right hand through her hair as he deepened the kiss, he swung his hands towards squeezing her plump ass. God, she tasted so good. The feel of her hips between his grasp and that intoxicating scent driving throughout his nose beckoned him on.

It intensified in a flash because all too soon he had her stripped, top off, dark green bra off, and her breasts on show. Hungrily, his lips took turns on each, biting on the best part, the cork at the end of a champagne bottle. Her response was stimulating to the ears; nobody could deny that, the way her body just roared with emotion.

Zack felt her fingers unbutton his shirt before impatiently moving on towards his buckle. Without warning, her lips were around his friend, scorching every possible part of him. As she sucked, he could do nothing but groan, dropping his head back as he gripped onto the sofa as the exhilaration of pleasure overwhelmed him.

He could have come in her mouth, but she pulled away all too soon. Zack had little time to think as she stripped off her jeans and stepped out of them wearing only her green lace knickers embroidered with red roses on the sides of the hips and began to tug at his trousers.

Eagerly, he took control, standing up as he grabbed her in his embrace and slipped his hands down her knickers to either side of her hips as well as kissing her lips to quench her lust. She was so desperate that she took no time, jumping on him to wrap her legs around his waist.

Carrying to her to the closest wall possible, which he soon realised was the window, given the condensation inflaming from behind her back, it did not stop either of them removing their final garments. Zack had no trouble removing her knickers, flicking them to the side like an elastic band, while all the while he held her firmly still against the window.

"*Zack…*" she breathed, combing her hands through his hair before gasping at the abrupt action of penetration finalising their desire. Thrust after thrust, she could feel her heart pounding uncontrollably as she felt impossibly overpowered by it all. How on earth the window managed to remain intact against the thudding movement was a mystery, the sound of hot, sweaty skin colliding against the cool surface.

Upstairs seemed more of a reasonable place to continue. His king-size bed, the sprawled duvet out on the floor and pillows thrown over the other side of the bed as she felt him grow only stronger as he picked up the pace. Every inch of him filled her entirely. Her fingertips burned on his skin, digging down onto his back and then clawing to his ass. Cries of ecstasy filled that room at its rawest. There was no trouble freeing herself as she felt her juices run wild across her thighs and mingle with his own.

It didn't stop there, and no sooner as he had her did he have her from the rear, to the side, and inflicting pure carnal growls as his tongue ran across her pussy lips.

Something had driven Claire to madness, but Zack for that moment could not complain. At that moment, all he could think of was her. How much he loved her, loved how she was here. That mind-blowing feeling from out of this world of having her under his fingertips. Nothing could explain it. So he couldn't argue.

Three a.m. Outside rain thundered, droplets meandering down the pane of the window, and in the distance, the sound of a few car alarms shrilling loud. Claire gently sighed as she looked towards the ceiling. She couldn't dwell on what had happened nor what she going to do but for that moment, she wanted to dream that everything between them was like the old times.

Shifting her head to the side, she admired the way he slept, his arm draped over his temple and the soft tempo of his breathing exiting his mouth. He was beautiful. Her heart stung with love for him, but she couldn't give it anymore justice.

Claire sat up, moving gently as she lifted herself up off the bed. She was completely exposed and had to be until she gathered up her clothes from downstairs. She couldn't stay.

Claire wanted him to feel conflicted. Perhaps she even wanted to feel cruel, insert the physical emotion of how it felt to be played. She just was too wrapped up in all these emotions that nothing appeared to make sense.

Taking a single glance back towards him as her hand lingered on the door handle, she pressed her lips together, feeling utterly ashamed but determined not to give in. As much as she wanted them, he had to understand it was for his own good. Their relationship was dead the second he'd told her who he was. And with that, she opened the door and left.

***

Zack yawned, stretching his arms out in front of him as he adjusted to the morning's brightness. He hesitated as he wondered if last night had really happened but was reassured when he felt it to be oddly breezy between his legs, and there was no way any of his other wet dreams could have beaten that affair.

Strangely, he was anxious and a bit excited to turn over and see her lying beside him. Perhaps it was because he thought they were making progress or he was just eager to know she was there. Several questions popped up in his mind: was she still asleep? Was she wide awake smiling at him or wondering the same:

had last night really happened? But when he turned over to his right, his smile instantly deflated, and the sight of an empty bed sat in his view.

Maybe she was downstairs? The bathroom?

He sighed, rubbing his temple as he sat up, scanning the room before laying his eyes at the centre of the bed at last night's stain of love. He wasn't imagining it then. Last night did happen. But where was Claire?

Grabbing a t-shirt from out of the wardrobe and slipping on some boxers to at least make a more reasonable entrance, Zak began to make his way downstairs, hoping again that he'd see her somewhere. It was another disappointment however when there was no one in the penthouse.

"Claire?" he said aloud, his naked feet slapping onto the wooden floor as he reached the bottom step. "You here?" Another walk around and still not a sign.

Why would she leave? Was she not even going to make the effort to discuss last night's incident? It pissed him off knowing she had gone up and left. They had sex. Surely, that made it more sense to talk things over.

There was a knock at the door, summoning his attention. With only a little ounce of hope left, he wondered if it was Claire returning back from some coffee shop holding bags of greasy bacon sandwiches, but when he opened the door, it was only his brother, Jared, and friend, Kyle, exiting the lift.

"Hey," Kyle said, slapping Zack's shoulder as he passed by. "*Rough* night?"

"Something like that," he mumbled, shutting the door behind Jared, who began to head for the fridge. "What are you two doing over here?"

"We thought since you're still moping about, you'd come out with us. We'll make a day of it," Kyle replied, thanking Jared as he passed him a bottle of beer. "Never too early for a beer. It's five o'clock somewhere in the world." He chuckled, clinking its neck to Jared's.

"Nah, I'm good. I got things to do," Zack dismissed, picking up his trousers from last night from off the floor. "Just—"

"Nah, *ah*," Kyle interrupted. "We aren't taking no for an answer. And I'd say you had *more* than a rough night. You had a battlefield in here. So where is she?" Kyle asked, analysing the room around him.

"Who?"

"Claire, I presume. I wouldn't think you moved on that quick from that woman," Kyle said before taking another swig of his drink. Jared agreed, nodding his head.

"Who fucking cares anymore?" Zack grumbled as he flopped onto the edge of the sofa. "Can you see her about? 'Cause I sure fucking can't." Swatting his hands away, he dropped his head in defeat, feeling utterly miserable.

"So it was Claire?" Jared reiterated.

"Who the fuck else do you think I slept with?" Zack snapped. "She came over, I thought we were going to talk, but instead she jumps on me. It's not like I was unaware how strange it was. But she was determined. And now, she's gone up and left." He was angered by the situation and how vulnerable it made him feel.

"Well, shit," Kyle cursed, lifting his brows up in shock. "That sucks. Why would—"

"Sex, I suppose," Zack spat, shaking his head. "I don't know. It just annoys me. I could be looking at all this wrong and she just felt ashamed or bad, but she could have left intentionally. I just thought she wanted to sort this out. Y'know? I was giving her time. And then she turns up last night, and fuck, she's giving me all these mixed messages."

"What you gonna do?" Jared asked.

"What can I do? She'll probably slam the door in my face when I try to go to speak to her," Zack said, kicking his feet onto the coffee table. "You know what? Let's just do whatever you were planning because I'm not cooping myself up in here all day."

"'Atta, boy!" Kyle enthused, slapping his knee.

CHAPTER FIFTEEN

Claire had spent the majority of her day with Darren, successful in persuading him to go to the park with her and get some fresh air. The rest of the day, she'd distracted herself from last night by grocery shopping.

Carrying the two bags of food, she balanced them as she inserted the front door key into the lock. She turned it but was startled by how the lock was already open. She was sure she locked up this morning.

A hundred percent certain that she had not left the door open, she crept inside and grabbed the nearest item—an umbrella.

Holding it up in defence, she slowly walked in, vigilant for any sudden attack from either side. Knowing the light switch was a patch of wall away from her, she took a deep breath, calculating her vulnerability as she readied herself to attack.

Then she switched the light on, and as her eyes caught sight of a figure sitting on the sofa wearing a black hoodie, she charged forward, screaming as she went in for the invasion.

"AHHHHHH!" she yelled, launching the umbrella to thump down onto their head. But seconds after the eruption of sound entered the apartment from her outburst, the figure turned, well aware of her presence, and grabbed the umbrella, stopping any ultimate damage it may or may have not caused.

"I'm gonna call the pol—" Claire cried, stopping short. "*Zack?*"

"Well, hello, *sweetheart*," he said, sarcasm dripping. "Where've you been?"

"What the hell, Zack?" She frowned, shamefully looking away from him as she dropped her keys onto the side table closest to the front door. "I thought someone was robbing the place, dickhead."

"And I thought I'd wake up finding a particular someone next to me this morning. But we can't always get what we want now, can we? Why did you leave, Claire? Why come over in the first place if you're just gonna get up and go?" he challenged as he dropped the umbrella onto the sofa.

"You're not supposed to be here."

"Where else am I *supposed* to be? Huh? You can't expect me to just accept the fact that you slept with me for digs because you sure as hell don't look bothered. And don't think I'll willingly go along with that." He paused, running his hand through his hair with frustration. "I love you, Claire, and I thought we were making progress. And yeah, okay…" He waved his hand about to make his point. "Sex doesn't solve the answer. But that's why you discuss things, not just up and go. So don't go pointing fingers."

"I'm not," Claire replied nonchalantly as she took off her coat and slipped it onto the coat hook. "So you can go now. Door is there." She pointed her index finger to the apartment door.

"Really?"

"Yes, *really*," Claire reiterated, pulling a face of exasperation as she picked up the shopping bags from outside the door.

"Oh, this is rich." Zack shook his head. "What? Have sex with me and push me aside? Like I don't mean anything to you? Huh? You can't just erase what we have. I don't know what you're trying to prove. Why are you being like this?" His tone dropped as he softly pleaded. "We could talk this through, *baby*."

"I don't care. So go."

Zack smirked lightly as he shook his head. "You *know*, Claire, you're just being a *dick* right now." He rubbed his hand against his slightly unshaven stubble. "I've done nothing but *apologised*, proven, or at least I thought I proved enough that I love you, and all you can do is fool me about." Sighing, he paced the little space of floor. "I'm trying to give you time. And here you are," he jabbed his finger at her, "complaining about me being here. Acting as if I don't suddenly mean anything to you when you showed up at my place. I lied, I know. Yet I'm owning up to my mistakes. I know what I want. It just seems like you're just creating the problem. Claire, you're just lying to yourself." He stormed towards the front door, slamming it on his way out.

CHAPTER SIXTEEN

Not a lot happened after Zack's abrupt exit. It felt as though like a murder had been committed when Claire shamefully glanced at the door, which acted as a lingering reminder of the damage she had caused. It might as well have been a murder, a literal gunshot. Gushing blood and the sudden darkness consuming the little life grasping on. She had completely destroyed Zack. Taken away what little hope he had for them.

Why did she do it? What had she accomplished except cause heartbreak for a man? But that's what she wanted. A sly move. Claire wanted to break him down, destroy his feelings for her. She had hoped that if she had left in the morning, Zack would have not batted an eyelid, unbothered by her disappearance. Yet to her dismay, he wasn't that easily let down. It appeared it wasn't a one-night stand for him, and as much as she wanted to agree to that, she couldn't allow those emotions to intoxicate her anymore. At this point, she just couldn't give anymore thought to their relationship; she wanted to forget it, mimic the exact purpose as an eraser.

Was it selfish? Yes, more than she had ever been. But she was hoping she was being selfish for him. He could do better, and she knew that. And then there was that insecurity motive again, her means of feeling unconfident if they were ever together. You could call Claire stupid or damn right ruthless, but she was concerned about both their appearances in all of this. What they would say about her and what they would say about him. She didn't want to ever feel put down, spoke of in such a manner that it destroyed her…and him? She wasn't in his elite circle. Who would understand that they fell in love without fingers pointing that she just wanted the stack of cash? It didn't matter if she was young or not; she wasn't in his league.

Claire thought it wouldn't have mattered after all when he admitted who he was and she wasn't put off. But seeing his place, knowing his position, and knowing all that time he'd known all along made her feel small. It sucked that all roads had led to this, but she was hoping she was being selfish for both of them.

Sunday mornings were usually blissful; she could get up at any time, trudge off to the gym if she wanted, or simply lay about in her pyjamas all day. At one point, she had Zack around here, his pure demeanour offering more than enough entertainment, and when they were together, a love she had twenty-four-seven in her pocket. Now, it was a different story. She felt disgusted in herself and not just by her groggy appearance, dribble plastered upon her chin and bags growing under her eyes from the lack of sleep last night.

Claire was annoyed with how she handled yesterday, after she thought when she turned up at his that perhaps everything would have been sorted and she'd been lying in his arms than at bay.

Rolling onto her side, she sighed. Everything would work out eventually. There was even the thought that perhaps she wouldn't even have her job. After all, she hurt the guy. What could she expect, though? She acted as if she never brushed a thought to him. Treated him like he was an accessory, a temporary fix to build up her walls, and then only to knock down his. Claire wanted to speculate how he felt, but she dismissed that thought as she sat up and shoved her feet into her slippers.

Part of her yearned to see his caller ID flashing onto her mobile screen when she picked it up off the side of her dresser. Nothing. Just what this new Claire was trying to feel for him.

Nothing appealed more than visiting Darren today, she couldn't risk staying alone in her thoughts. It would eat her up, and besides, Darren had it ten times worse, that constant reminder of his loss shoved in his face. She needed more than ever to be there for him than mope in her own thoughts.

So, with determination, Claire got changed, putting on a pair of skinny jeans and pairing it with an old, green baggy t-shirt. As far as it came to hair, she shoved it into a ponytail, hoping the obvious greasiness it had obtained from the miss of two days' wash would do it justice.

It took her perhaps little more than an hour to get to Darren's block of flats after a minor accident on the road plunged the traffic into congestion. After climbing the first set of stairs, she headed down the corridor, offering a sympathetic glance towards Jonas's door that was plastered with cards of condolences, and at its foot, rows of flowers ranging from white and pink lilies to dark red roses. At least there was sympathy for him.

Taking a deep breath, Claire attempted a smile, working on making it appear natural as she knocked on the door. She had to put on a brave face for Darren. He needed her more than ever, and it would be selfish to focus on her own problems.

She could hear the locks being shifted on the

other side until eventually the door opened. At first sight, Darren was cleanly shaven, something that surprised her. His clothes appeared fresher and cleaner, brown shirt and pair of blue washed jeans, but what took her more in shock was the towering cardboard boxes sat at either side of the corridor behind him.

Claire's eyes pulled with scrutiny as she asked, "Everything *okay*?"

Darren slowly nodded, moving aside as she entered his apartment and continued to examine every crevice and item she could get a look at. "I'm just in the middle of things. I didn't expect to see you. Usually, you're still *lounging* about in your pyjamas. I know what you do on a Sunday morning. Something sparked you up with energy today?" he said. She noted the absence of that hoarse, weak whisper she had grown used to. Claire even acknowledged his conversational tone but dismissed it towards what she was really implying.

"Darren, what is with all *these* boxes? They...Jonas's th—"

"No," Darren said, walking on ahead of Claire as he headed into the central living room, which looked as bare as the corridor felt, despite the heavy packing of boxes. "You were *supposed* to come around later, or rather I was going...to tell you *later*." Itching his head awkwardly, he sat on the sofa that was missing the bright pink blanket that had given it life.

"What's happening?" Claire muttered, her voice on edge as she slowly sat down in the armchair opposite the two-seater.

Darren exhaled. "I'm moving, Claire."

"W-what?" she whispered, her voice failing to remain distinctly audible.

Her friend nodded his head, failing to meet her eyes for a few seconds until confidently he looked up and explained, "Yeah. I'm moving to London. You know when I told you about that list that Jonas made when he got his promotion? Well, we had it down as moving to London, you know, so…" He nervously licked his bottom lip. "I want to follow his wish, our wish. And you were right; the company can transfer me to their base over there or…I could just do something else. I just need to go, Claire."

Claire's bottom lip quivered as she rubbed her palms together. "I know this is selfish to say, but what about me? I don't know what I'll do without you, Darren. You're…my best friend. My family."

Darren smiled weakly. "And you're mine. I've thought about it hard, and it's just something I have to do. I feel trapped here, Claire. Everything is too depressing, so I need to make the move. And you know you're always welcome to visit me," Darren explained, leaning forward as he grabbed Claire's hand. "If anything, I'll be homesick missing you, and I'll be begging you to come over every weekend."

Claire couldn't hold back the tears, not this time. This just wasn't what she had expected. He was her everything. All those memories. The countless laughs in the kitchen at work, the movie nights on weekends, and how they had each other's back scoping for that cute guy in the club. If anything, this felt worse than when Abbey left. Ten times more. She was closer to Darren since day one.

"Girl, hottie five o'clock to ya," Darren whispered, drawing Claire's attention to the right. "He's totally working those eyes up and down at you. He's got those 'fuck me, mommy' eyes."

Claire laughed rolling her eyes, "Yuck, Darren!"

Another flashback.

"Are you sure?" she whimpered, wiping back the tears running down her cheeks.

"Yes." He nodded. "I have the apartment sorted, work, and I'll have you always on dial. My mother will visit when she can, and it will be a chance to start something new, knowing Jonas is always at my step."

Claire sobbed, shaking her head as she closed the gap between them and hugged her arms around him. "I'm just…going to m-miss you so much. I love you so, so much." She choked on the load of tears. "B-but as l-long a-as you're happy, that's—that's all that matters." Kissing the side of his neck, she tightened her embrace around him.

"I love you too, babes," Darren croaked, holding his best friend close. "We'll never be far from each other. Not really. You know that?"

Claire nodded, weeping into his neck.

"Darren! The film's going to start in a second. Get your ass over here!" Claire bellowed out into the corridor.

"Err, excuse me, honey!" Darren remarked, exiting from the bathroom with his face covered in some green facial mask and his pink dressing gown he'd once bought from a charity shop. "Beauty doesn't wait for anyone. I gotta look hot."

The memories just seemed endless.

Darren pulled Claire back as he swiped his thumbs against her cheeks to remove the falling tears. "And *you*? I'd feel better if you told me that situation with you and Zack was sorted. So is everything okay between you two now?"

"Yes," Claire lied, sniffling as she sat beside him.

"Don't lie," Darren warned. "I know when you're lying."

Claire pressed her lips together as she

dropped her head back, blinking back more tears as she spoke, her tone weak and full of despair. "I messed up, Darren…I had no choice. It just won't work between us. I slept with him Friday, and all I could do was wave it off as nothing to him. I want him to hate me because it will make it all easier."

Darren tutted, shaking his head as he intertwined his fingers through her left hand. "Darling, what are you doing? This man loves you. Why should it matter whether he's rich? And you know without a doubt he loves you. All that lying shouldn't mean a shit to you. He loves you, and that's all that should matter."

"But, but—"

"No, Claire," Darren interrupted, squeezing her hand. "You're a fool if you're gonna give up that easily. Why care if a few stuck-up brats say a word or two? What should matter is you have each other, and that is all. And you know?" He paused as he took a shaky breath. "You're lucky. I would do anything to have Jonas here with me." Claire felt ashamed as she acknowledged how abusive she'd been to something so precious that Darren had lost.

"Look," Darren began. "Don't give up. Please. If that's one thing I want to be sure of before I leave this place, it's that you're happy, too." Then with a light chuckle he added, "Stop being so fucking stubborn, Claire. Would you? Please."

Claire sniffled weakly, turning into him for another hug as she muttered a word of apology and pondered quietly to herself what Darren had said to her.

"Promise me," Darren demanded, pulling Claire away again.

"I promise." She nodded, ever so grateful she had a friend like him; he was irreplaceable.

CHAPTER SEVENTEEN

Rodeo in Central Park was the name of that book. Sold 2.5 million copies all across the world for its sensational, vibrant romance stirring the population of middle-aged women who yearned for a sex life just as depicted in all fifty-five chapters. It was a great read. Corny, but something that couldn't be put down. Claire, however, just felt disappointed with the protagonist of the story, some business-class woman who couldn't help but be as stubborn as possible over denying her feelings for a Texas cowboy. There couldn't have a been a bolder sign to show that man's love, yet her deliberate ignorance was always getting in the way. And because of that, this woman was near to losing all contact with her fella who boarded a plane back on to sunny ol' Texas, struggling to put up a fight for their relationship. That was how frustrating she had become. Like many other

221

readers, Claire disliked how long it took for this woman to depart from her old ways and realise her love for this man. Perhaps that was what made it more realistic. Strange how that story was suddenly feeling familiar to that of her own. Was she as foolish as that woman? Because she could sure as hell remember the drop-dead, gorgeous cowboy vexed by how the woman he loved was suddenly treating him. There was more than enough resemblance to her own situation, a difficult person like herself and a fed-up Zack, tired of waiting around.

Then there was her other issue: Darren was leaving. It had of course been discussed before, in response towards Jonas's promotion. That, Claire could remember, but at least she knew her friend wouldn't have been moving alone. Now, it just seemed apparent that he wanted to leave everything behind, depressed by how every little thing reminded him of his late lover. It was understandable, yet as much as she listened to him speak so passionately of needing to do this for himself, Claire couldn't just allow him to go.

It was heartbreaking to think that the man she had known for three and half years would no longer be in easy reach. How on earth was it going to be possible to not picture Darren sitting opposite her at work? Claire would miss him terribly, that pink-feathered pen stuck between his lips and the hidden smirk he attempted to disguise, prominent even as he ducked down below the desktop as he made a remark; whether he was teasing Claire about her sexual life or bitching his latest on Monica. God, Claire was even certain she missed Monica now, only because it became the sole topic on Darren's lips. Who else would provide her the humour, gossip, and protection that Darren had given? Sure, she could visit and talk over the phone, but it just didn't feel the same as meeting face to face each day. It made no sense without Darren. And there was no sense in finding a stranger's face opposite than the man she called her friend. It felt like the sun was being cast away for a ship of rain.

What on earth was she going to do?

It was raining outside. Typical Sunday evening. Typical British weather. She had already attempted to call Abbey, hoping her old friend and roommate would at least provide comfort, but for whatever reason, she wasn't available to take the call, and there was her attempt to phone her dad, who answered but wasn't there beside Claire to physically console her as he tried to do over the phone.

"Dad, what do I do?" She sniffled, holding the grey-stuffed cushion against her chest as she looked out the window. From all that she had told him, he had told her sincerely the truth.

"Claire," he began, muting the volume on the television in the background. "Just be yourself now. Stop holding yourself back. Stop being so afraid. Make things right; that's all you can attempt to do. Ignore those feelings that pull you back and just take a chance." An encouraging tone that offered slight hope.

And as for the rest of the evening, Claire was left to dive into her thoughts. She felt so alone. Claire wanted so desperately to have Zack beside her, pulling her into his arms as he rocked her quietly asleep. She was so scared. It just didn't shock her then when she spoke reassuringly to herself, an act of madness, hoping somehow somebody would reply. More importantly, Zack.

Voicemail after voicemail, she'd left him a dozen after each one was left to ring out. She poured her heart out into everything, hoping that if he was actually listening, he'd pick up the phone and answer. But he didn't, nor did she expect him to after she'd broken his heart.

Darren was right. He was always right. How she had handled the situation was not a smart move, and instead she had only abused something so precious that he had been deprived of. She knew she had to fix it. She knew she couldn't keep lying to herself as Zack had pointed out.

"Zack," she would begin, trying her hardest to hold back tears as she watched the rain clatter upon adjacent roofs. "I'm so, so sorry. I didn't mean to hurt you...I never meant to...I j-just wanted to…" Then she would stop, end the call, and cry as she wondered whatever had possessed her to punish Zack.

The rain picked up speed, hammering down onto the metallic roofs of cars forming a symphony of sound; each pitter patter down the window pane mimicked how Claire felt. She deserved this pain. It could have been prevented, but she summoned it.

"Zack," she would then weep, wondering if this would be the call he'd answer. Her knuckles faded whiter as she gripped onto the phone. "I'm sorry. I love you so much. I know that. I've a-always known that from the second I saw you…p-please forgive me." Then she would end that voicemail and ring out again, and then again, and then again until finally fatigue washed entirely over her and she was left to fall into the hands of sleep.

***

Monday made no difference. It didn't matter that she was at a keyboard; it didn't matter that she had deadlines or the fact she had to rely on it for next month's rent. It just didn't matter anymore.

A, B, E, backspace, backspace. God, Claire couldn't even manage to spell a simple word; her mind just seemed more jumbled up as seconds climbed on. Everyone around her was all oblivious, trapped in their own bubbles, whilst Claire felt darkness consume her in utter misery. She wanted to breathe again, and deep down she knew the answer to that lay with Zack. Oh, how she expected him to walk through the department at any second, glance over at her with confidence, before racing over to her to then lift her in his arms with glory. Claire wanted to feel his arms wrap around her and hear him say that everything would be all right. She wanted it more than anything. The weekend had been such a foolish mistake.

Why hadn't he phoned back?

Fuck, fuck, and fuck, Claire cursed as she shook her head and fell defeatedly into her arms.

"Excuse me, Claire." A voice caught her attention; it was in haste, as suspected by the several times she heard the woman exhale. Sitting up and turning in her desk chair, she acknowledged it was one of her colleagues, Kate, a single, young mother she had spoken to a couple of times. "Sorry, so sorry, but I am going to be a pain and ask if you could finish off the copies I've sent to the printer. My son has been sick at school, and I need to go pick him up. Is that okay?" she explained, pushing her brown handbag's strap further onto her shoulder uncomfortably.

Claire nodded her head. "Sure, not a

problem. You go check on your son. Go, go, go," Claire said with a sympathetic smile, soon standing up as she headed towards the giant machine that served at least eight functions, including photocopying. At least it would take her mind off things if she had something else productive to do.

Leaning on the machine, she sighed and out of boredom began to read the posters stuck above it on the wall. Each one went on about punctuality, the right attitude, and teamwork. Claire frowned, turning her attention towards the huge stack of papers freshly printed coming out the right end of the towering giant. By what it said on the interactive screen, she had another hundred copies to go. How on earth was that going to keep her distracted?

"How much longer you got?"

Andrew, who usually sat across from Susan-the-office-gossiper, stood ahead of her as he swung his ID pass between his fingers. Claire replied shortly, "Ages."

"Ah, really?" he complained, stomping his left foot on the floor as he leaned back. "The other one is still being repaired. Oh, well." He sighed, lifting his ginger, fair brows. "Just hold it for me when you finish. I don't want another bugger getting it before me. I would wait, but I must send a couple of emails to some clients. Be a darling and hold it for me?" Andrew could have had a bloody knife between his fingers and yet she'd still say yes to him. He had this award-winning puppy face that just accentuated his adorable smile, and the dozen odd freckles he had made him only appear more juvenile. It did make her feel all protective, like she was cradling a puppy in her arms, threatened by the intimidating world.

"Okay," she exhaled, giving a thumbs up as she leaned back onto the machine. "I'll just wave you over when I'm done."

"Thanks, Claire. You're a star," he said, smiling as he began to turn on his heel. "Oh, do you know where that fella went? Zack? I figured you know 'cause he's your roommate, isn't he? I'm just curious. After all, he is missing work. He got the man flu or something? Susan had a bet he secretly is following Monica all the way to Milan, like he's going to offer his services when the old man can't. Because boy, I don't have a clue on how she's going to manage that old bag pushing his weight onto her." Andrew snorted.

Claire pressed her lips tightly together, wishing she could have dodged a question like this. "I actually don't know where he is. He...moved out recently," she lied, her eyes looking at the floor rather than his face. "I think he just didn't like the job."

"Ah, really? That sucks. He was good to talk to. And I'm not gonna lie but..." Andrew paused as he stepped forward. "But if I *was* gay,

I'd totally have a mean crush on the guy. He was just so intimidating and confident, a real man," he whispered, nodding as he pulled back. "Well, I better go send those emails. Again, thanks, Claire." Before he headed on over to the far blocks, Claire could see he'd immediately transferred the information to Susan. That woman just had a knack for snooping her nose into everything.

After retrieving the copies from the machine and then holding it for Andrew to take over, Claire was just about exhausted as she headed for lunch. She had about seven emails that needed to be addressed, an incomplete design sent to her from a co-worker who meekly asked for her help, and a paragraph that was at a deadline, which needed to be assessed for grammatical errors before it could be sent off towards the publishers. Being in the Sales and Marketing department for three years, not once had Claire been this sloppy on getting her work done. Now, she was making a sloth look as fast as Usain Bolt.

Her day got even worse when her favourite café ran out of her preferred baguette filling of spicy meatballs. The ham and cheese sandwich just did not look appetising as she fiddled with the tissue under it at one of the single two-man tables. What next? She'd forget her bag, leave it here for a lucky thief to take? She could only hope her coffee was still piping hot.

Claire glanced outside, observing the swarm of people passing by just out of boredom until she swore she caught sight of Zack passing hastily by. Without needing a reason to remain seated, she grabbed her bag and jogged out the café, swerving through the several people heading in as she exited the establishment.

Outside was a different story, and without at least being six feet tall, she couldn't see a damn thing. "Zack!" she dared to shout, pushing through the crowd as she scanned each possible male, hoping it would be him.

"Zack!"

"Hey, lady, watch where you're going!" a man barked as she accidentally bumped into him.

Without bothering to stop and apologise, she pushed on, eventually seeing a peek of black tousled hair through the gap of people, where he had stopped ahead at the curb waiting for the traffic lights to give pedestrians permission to cross. "Zack!" she called again, hoping somehow he would hear and turn around. At once, she shot away from the crowd and headed straight for him.

"Zack, Zack...I'm—" She tapped his shoulder to get his attention.

But when the man turned around, he was not a in any way similar to Zack.

"Can I help you?"

Claire shook her head. "*Sorry*, I—sorry."

Then she turned back, taking only a single glance as she watched the man blink in confusion and continue with his day as he crossed the road. She felt suddenly more alone, trapped, and it didn't help as people shoved and pushed by as she stood in the middle of the path, frozen.

By the time she reached her department floor, her lunch hour was officially over, and just as she expected, Graves, who was one to usually make his inspection, caught her exiting the lift.

"Claire." He shook his head. "I didn't expect this tardy behaviour from you. I'm going to have to warn you by recording this on your file as late."

Claire didn't breathe a word as she slouched over to her desk where even with the threat of deadlines nagging her, she remained inattentive. Everything was just going to hit the fan.

CHAPTER EIGHTEEN

In the space of two weeks, a lot of shit had happened. If somebody had told Zack that he'd be actually eating a pint of Ben and Jerry's as he moped over the current situation with Claire, he would have laughed. It would have seemed impossible for the old Zack who knew only that a woman in his bed was the night's comfort.

But this shit was actually happening. He was actually stuffing his mouth with vanilla ice cream, scooping it out with the large metal spoon that was ideally supposed to be used for dishing out large portions of meals like lasagna, not ice cream.

"You know you have over seventeen voicemails on your phone?" Kyle expressed, regarding the flashing alerts springing onto Zack's mobile phone that sat on the side table. Zack dismissed the comment, shovelling another mouthful of ice cream as he simultaneously turned up the sound on the television.

"Zack?" Kyle repeated, responding to Zack's ignorance. "Oi, dickhead!" He threw a cushion against his shoulder, hoping that it would do the trick to gather Zack's full attention.

"What?" he snapped, placing his ice cream to the side. "I really don't want to hear it, Kyle. It can stay with over seventeen notifications. I really couldn't give a fuck. Now, will you shut up and let me watch my action movie in peace? I'm going to miss the best part again because of you." Sitting himself back, he kicked his feet onto the coffee table ahead.

"Well, what if it's important? What if she needs you?" Kyle persisted, ignoring Zack's previous comment. Kyle was no idiot. He could see that his friend was upset, and as much as he would have liked to rejoice in a bitching session about the woman, he also knew that Claire was someone who made Zack happy. It had to be a mistake.

"I doubt that, Kyle. You know if I needed a therapist, I would have called one, but I don't," Zack bitterly said. "We're not discussing that name ever again. I'm over it. You should be happy; we can hit the clubs like we used to. I can bring whoever back and I won't have to worry about being tied down." His tone was assertive, which scared Kyle the most.

"I'm not happy about that, Zack. And you

233

can't think it's over. It has to be a silly mistake," Kyle objected, shaking his head before he lifted the can of cider to his lips. "I—" He paused before he took a sip. "I don't want to see you so unhappy, Zack. You need Claire and she needs you. Bullshit on what she preached the other day." Then he took a long swig.

"I hate that I fell in love," Zack muttered, running his hands slowly through his hair. "It has just caused trouble. So just shut up with all your love bullshit. I don't want to hear it," he warned, and for the rest of Monday night, that was that. He didn't want to hear her, speak to her, or see her again.

Funny how one person could change your life. He was so used to that high-life—the one that knew no limits—and until he fell in love, he thought having the freedom to be with whoever and do whatever wouldn't be possible if he was tied in a relationship. Zack was proved wrong on that. But now he wasn't so sure. Nothing made sense. He couldn't even be sure if Claire actually loved him anymore. That night when she told him she didn't care, didn't need him or want him, frightened him. It was that possibility that he was more than alone. It pushed fear through his veins. He had admitted to someone besides his mother that he loved someone, and to have it thrown back in his face destroyed him.

Zack had always used women. There was no sugar-coating that. When he wanted that woman who was shimmying her hips in the nightclub or deliberately grinding her body upon him, he used her. No matter if he was intoxicated or sober, he saw fit that there were mutual feelings even before hitting the bed that they were using one another for that moment's affection. But that was a terrifying thought now. It was sensible to think that he really was alone. And not once had he dared given a thought to if that other person fell for him. It never crossed his mind. It just wouldn't make sense to tie himself down. So, like he had done many times, he'd left or told them to when things became complicated.

How strange things had changed. With Claire, he had grown with confidence on sharing his feelings, allowing himself to be entirely exposed and given to this mad thing called love. But now part of him felt lost and fearful without Claire. He didn't know how to handle love. What was he supposed to do with it now? It scared him because it made him more vulnerable. No question about it.

He wasn't going to listen to those voicemails; he wasn't going allow himself to be broken any further, for he was too afraid to succumb to emotion. He needed to reacquaint himself with his old self. Forget Claire. Move on. Come to think of it, he had the power to physically detach Claire, but he wouldn't do that. Heck, he had the money to force her to move herself out of his life, but he couldn't. For now, he had to focus on work, focus on himself, and work on bettering himself in the world he was a part of. He couldn't live a life like he'd had, and he would have to learn to grow up, tackle the real world. By the end of this week, the magazine would be out; it would confirm his place as CEO, rid all those weak stories on his romantic affairs, and instead concrete him as a real man of business. No messing about. He couldn't dally any longer with triviality. Claire had made it clear. She wasn't a part of his life.

***

Tuesday had been a little simpler. Zack was a little more convinced he was regaining that old part of him. He had woken up refreshed, determined, and ready to face the world. He'd made it clear to Kyle last night that such things shouldn't be spoken around him and had made the man promise that tonight they would venture out to the club, creating peace in his mind.

As for today, he had to remain hidden from work. He wanted to reveal his true identity to the department he'd been undercover with by Thursday, and then he could go back to his world properly. He had yet to organise a final meeting, one that he wanted his father to be included in to see his development in full swing. The sustainable homes he had vouched for were underway, and construction had been given word as early as this morning, providing a few paycheques already from those clients who desired to be in sustainable living. Wednesday would be the finale; it would be the moment he'd weaken his father. Why? Olivia had already pitched him a few comments on the project from the analysts on this moment's success rate. He had the project in the bag, and despite previous remarks on how it would only achieve half, it seemed more successful than they thought. Some would say Zack's exhilaration was out of denial, but to him, he was feeling like a man who had a grip on the world.

Every step felt lighter; he felt entirely more pleased when he glanced at the man looking right back at him in the mirror. He looked confident as someone he'd remembered seeing only a few months back being. There looked like there was no weakness. How odd that one night suddenly made an abrupt difference.

Zack trekked downstairs, self-assured with his progress as he poured himself coffee brewed by his maid, who'd returned from her holiday only yesterday. The flavour tickled his taste buds as he gasped with delight, closing his eyes as he wondered if he'd been cured from the madness that was love and been gifted to his old self.

He was more energetic, collecting his phone and keys and stuffing them in his suit jacket. He didn't even give a second glance to the several more notifications on his screen joining those that remained unheard. Zack even managed a spring in his step towards the front door as he headed into the lift to the underground garage.

It was there he was greeted with the two rows of cars, each one with their own personality and style, that he became only more indulged in happiness as he stroked the bonnet of his red Lamborghini.

"I'll think I'll take you for a ride for today." He smiled to himself as he drew over to the cabinet and retrieved the keys to the car he'd selected. Something oddly bizarre was going on, but for all he cared, he wasn't complaining about this joy.

The drive to work was also carefree. The radio station was playing his favourite songs, traffic lights appeared to always remain on green, and there was no congestion as he pulled up behind his establishment, dodging any unwanted attention. He still had to play it safe until all could be revealed.

Stepping out of his car and locking it effortlessly, Zack exhaled, pleased that he was radiating self-assurance and boldly making a stance on his two feet. He could have skipped inside the building, but instead, still on that similar vibe, he took long strides to the confidential lift installed at the back. He could even vouch how terribly vain he felt, the natural sexiness and his expensive navy blue suit accompanied with his charming smile. At this rate, he felt like he could own the world.

"Good morning, Olivia," Zack announced as he entered his office. "Make record that there is to be a meeting in relation to the project's development, and I require the attendance of the one and only Elijah Benson for tomorrow in the glass conference room. Also, if you could be a doll and grab me a coffee, that would be great. Thank you." He entered his complex office that appeared to be collecting dust since he'd been gone.

Taking hostage of the leather desk chair, Zack flopped himself in it, smiling as he turned it around and wheeled it to the large glass windows. He could breathe. Smell. Taste. And from today, he had the right to not give a damn.

Around three o'clock in the afternoon, Zack was still burning on those fumes. He was still energetic, not an ounce of sadness as he left the board room, finalising entirely the transfer of cash towards his project. He was heading for home, knowing he couldn't do a lot more than risk showing his face and so was satisfied he could take an early trip out.

Heading down the stairs rather than taking the lift and feeling more than ever in shape, he took the long descent, knowing that he had far to go but wasn't allowing anything of the sort to rain on his parade.

Around the eighth floor, but he wasn't exactly certain, Zack, who was entirely zoned out, remained oblivious to somebody shouting out his name.

"Zack!" someone cried out. He could hear frantic footsteps chasing him downstairs. "Zack, please. Stop!" Wheezing for breath, he refused to stop. It was only when a hand clamped down on his shoulder that he turned and the confidence he felt dispersed as quickly as he felt he regained it this morning.

Claire, who was struggling to hold her breath, sniffled as she wiped away the wet tears from her cheeks as she exhaled with desperation. "P-please, Zack. Why wouldn't you stop? You haven't answered my calls."

Zack bit down on his tongue, feeling that overwhelming tide of wreckage fatally overcoming him. Instead, he chose to crush it, dismissing her anguish as he calmly said, "Miss Winter, you need to be careful running downstairs. You could get hurt. It's Mr. Benson or sir to you. You better be getting back to your work. Otherwise you'll be faced with disciplinary action. I wouldn't want to have to page Mr. Graves. Excuse me." He slid past her.

"What?" Claire gaped, blinking as she tried to grip onto his arm. "Zack, what are you talking about? Zack!" she cried, watching as he refused to answer and continued hurriedly downstairs, accompanied with a whistle of tune. "Zack! Zack!"

It must be a sign of madness salvaged from the thought of denial. That part of him that wanted to hear her, hold her, kiss her, and have every part of her was trying hard to free itself, but for some apparent reason, Zack refused to allow himself to be vulnerable.

Claire couldn't understand what happened; she couldn't even push herself to carry on as she refused to believe that the man she loved had dismissed her entirely. He'd looked her in the eyes and treated her like a stranger. She had been out on the stairwell, exactly at the place where she and Zack shared their first kiss, that instant moment where sparks flew. She'd been there about ten minutes, moping, until she saw him coming downstairs, oblivious to her presence until she'd captured his arm. And now, he'd left without a word of anger, consolation, or love. It was like he was lost, entirely gone.

Her fault. She'd completely broken him. She could see that now. Claire wished he'd shown anger, cursed at her, or spoke a few words of dismay and not entirely washed her away. But that's what she did, wasn't it? Only she'd wounded the man.

Helpless, Claire fell to her knees, sobbing as she pushed her hand up against her face. What was she supposed to do? How was she going to fix this?

***

Kyle was hesitant as he picked up Zack from his penthouse, wary that his friend wasn't exactly behaving his "normal" self. It was proved by how he'd watched Zack unashamedly flirt with Kyle's female helicopter instructor earlier this afternoon. He'd had no guilt pushing back a strand of hair or whispering intimately against her ear.

He didn't want to take him out tonight. He was afraid he'd do something he'd regret, so he had Jared tag along, who was also voicing the same concern as soon as he saw the overly thrilled behaviour his brother was flaunting.

"Well, my fellas, great night to get laid." Zack laughed as he slapped Kyle on the back as he put the car into motion. "What the fuck is wrong with you, Kyle? You look like you had a dick slapped across your face. Cheer up, would you?"

"Zack," Jared warned from the backseat of the car.

"What the fuck is wrong with you? Jeez, I'm starting to think you haven't had sex for quite some while. Let's just get to this club. So, step on it, Kyle," Zack said, motioning his hand forward as he adjusted his seatbelt more comfortably.

As soon as they arrived, Kyle was cautious to get out of the car. It just wasn't Zack, and nor could his friend vouch that he was his old self when this wasn't even him. Heck, he was wild into affairs, but he wasn't entirely irresponsible. Not even the bouncer at the door was convinced his friend was sober enough to enter, but with more encouraging—particularly cash, that problem was solved.

Inside, neon pink and green lights lit the complex space up, and bass music blasted from each stereo. Some exclusive DJ was there, remixing classic tunes that thundered plenty of people to the centre of the dance floor or unmindfully dancing at the bar. Kyle, who normally wasn't so uptight, already had four females grind their bodies up against him as he passed through, but his voice of concern was for Zack.

"Jared, I'll get us some drinks. You get Zack to the VIP section without hassle," Kyle instructed loudly as he challenged the volume of the music.

Jared nodded. "Okay." His figure disappeared through the crowd as silhouettes mashed into shapes from the dozen or so dancing that barricaded the entrance to the upstairs area.

With time, it took him a while to order three drinks, instructed to be delivered upstairs from the clatter of people surrounding the bar. He could have just ordered upstairs without effort, but anxiety was biting at the best of Kyle, and he just couldn't face seeing his friend odd.

Once upstairs, he took notice to how Jared was nowhere to be seen, and Zack was preoccupied with the woman he had situated on his lap with his hands squeezing her ass. Kyle shook his head, somewhat angered. Part of him felt part to blame for all of this, and much of him wanted to own up by ensuring that Zack didn't do something he regretted. His friend was a fool if he shut Claire out.

"Zack," Kyle shouted over the music, looking around and noticing a group of women laughing by the balcony taking glimpses at Kyle. Any other time, he would have gladly made himself known, but his friend needed his help. "Zack, can we talk?"

Zack smirked, stroking his thumb across the woman's cheek as he leaned in to kiss her lips and greedily kneaded his hands upon her body as he brought her in.

"Zack." He heard his name and complied after only a second.

"What?" he yelled over the music as he allowed the woman to scoot off his lap.

"Can we talk?"

Kyle pressed forward, ushering the woman to him as he quickly swiped a couple of notes into her hand, discreet enough that he hoped Zack didn't see. "Go," he ordered her and watched as she sashayed away, soon forgetting her previous encounter as she whooped to the music. Probably barely sober.

"Where's she going?" Zack grimaced, the neon lights flashing across his shirt and face, revealing the cover of sweat against his forehead.

"Zack, you shouldn't be here," Kyle called over, dismissing his question. "You should be at home. Claire—"

"Don't you fucking bring this up!" Zack yelled back, his voice only just barely being heard over the loud, vibrant music deafening their eardrums. "Now, stop being such a bore. I'm gonna go find that girl." He stood up, stalking out the booth and pushing across the slim walkway to the stairs, but was stopped when Kyle held his shirt.

"No, I can't let you," Kyle said firmly, not at all the slightest comfortable with the way it suddenly became more tense between the pair. At the side of him, he could hear Jared returning, warning Zack the same.

"You can't say what I can and can't do," Zack threatened, glaring at Kyle.

"You can't, Zack. You'll regret it," Jared inputted.

"Shut up!" Zack barked, shoving Kyle's hand off him. "Fuck off the both of you." Pushing on ahead, he was stopped when Kyle grabbed onto his shoulder. Without thinking, Zack turned ferociously around and threw a punch into Kyle's face.

The rest went down in a blur, masked by the pumping music and hidden lights.

Zack whimpered as he turned onto his side but restrained from doing so as he felt his right hand clamped down on something. Opening his eyes, he registered that he was back home, and it had still not shifted to another day as seen by the night sky.

"You're awake then?" he heard someone say. It was Kyle holding a bag of peas to his nose as he sat on the edge of the sofa on the end by Zack's feet. Jared was also here too, flicking through the television with the remote.

"What happened?" Zack asked, dazed by the situation.

"You threw a punch; that's what you did. We had to restrain you and get you out of there before you made any more damage. Oh, and we're banned from there now. So..." Kyle shrugged his shoulders as he pressed the bag harder onto his nose. "You fell asleep, and well, you're awake now."

"I punched you? Man, I'm sorry," Zack muttered, lifting himself up. "I honestly don't even know what overcame me. Damn, what was

I even thinking? I was going to sleep with that woman, wasn't I?"

Kyle nodded quietly.

"Shit."

"But you didn't, so you can stop stressing. As for this situation with Claire, it will work its way out. Just don't fuck it up anymore," Kyle commented as he pulled the bag away from his red, sore nose. Patches of blood could be seen around the rim of his nostril where the impact must have broken through the skin.

"I know," Zack sighed, slumping his shoulders. "Hey, thanks, both of you. I'm going crazy and you guys are here for me. I appreciate it. Sorry about your nose again, Kyle," he apologised.

"It's fine." Kyle waved off.

"Y'know," Zack began as he rubbed the back of his head, "I thought I was being my old self today. I felt oddly happy and careless. I saw her today…and I totally blew her off."

Jared switched off the television. "Zack, that wasn't you, brother. All of this should be proof that you and Claire can't be separate. You're in this too deep to call it quits." He stood up and headed on over towards his brother. "It will all work out eventually…just stay out of trouble," he advised then patted Zack on the shoulder. "I'm off. C'mon, Kyle."

Zack nodded, thanking them both as he wondered what on earth had consumed him today. He couldn't even remember what was going on for the half of it.

And Claire? He just didn't know how to feel. Part of him was still angered by last weekend's affair. Yet today, as much as he could remember, she was begging for his attention. Was it out of love or a sly act? He just didn't know. Claire had really hurt him.

CHAPTER NINETEEN

There had to be a solution, a logical and apparent cause; Zack must have hit his head and suffered an episode of temporary amnesia. Claire shook her head as she flipped the chicken over in the frying pan; that of course was not the answer as she wholeheartedly knew. No, Zack was heartbroken. At this rate, it just seemed to be a never-ending cycle. He barked, then she barked, and nothing was mending the broken pieces together. Did that mean something bad? Claire just didn't have a clue anymore.

As for yesterday, her encounter with Zack threw her into an ocean of loss for the rest of that day, meaning she hadn't managed a lot of work. It was a struggle to also keep a brave face on, for one, and if she hadn't already been getting threatening emails from Graves about her tardy progress, she might have broken down in front of the whole office. Luckily, she'd held herself together until she got back home and then broke into a whirlwind of emotion without a crowd of spectators.

And Wednesday? It had been pretty much the same. Although at least she managed one sentence. That was some progress. If anything, that ticked one goal off her piling list of things to do.

Now, a meal for one seemed more appetising than the day she had.

Darren was one of her dilemmas. After work, she'd decided to head on over, fixated on the hope that he changed his mind, but that soon deflated when she saw the same cardboard boxes stacked up in the corners of the corridor.

"How much more you got to pack?" Claire asked, biting her tongue as she handed him a tower of CDs.

"Well," he contemplated, taking the CDs out of her hands as he placed them into a small box, marked on the left side with permanent black marker as "BEDROOM." "I'm leaving at the end of this week, so I'd say I have until the end of this week. I'm leaving all the stuff I'm still using to last, and I have the rented van coming tomorrow, so…" Darren clicked his tongue at the roof of his mouth. "I can move all the heavy stuff into that, and then, well, that leaves me with not a lot to pack. So all is on target."

Claire nodded, absentmindedly staring at the

red blanket upon his bed, recalling the countless times they'd watched midnight movies or straight-out bitched about Monica at work. It was also that spot where Claire vomited when she witnessed that horrific video Darren had shown her on his phone. She wasn't going to go into detail with that.

"And you?" Darren asked, dragging her back to reality.

She blinked several times.

"Have you done what I said?"

Claire shrugged her shoulders as she flopped down onto the edge of his bed. "I have...I mean, I've tried."

"Like?"

"I sent him voicemails, and...I saw him yesterday," she mumbled, hoping that was enough to drift Darren from interrogating her further. But this was Darren she was talking about, and this man had no means of not being persistent.

"And? Everything cool now?" Darren questioned, dropping the odd bits and bobs into the box.

"No," Claire replied, short with her answer. "It isn't."

Darren sighed, shoving the box further onto his dresser as he then walked over and sat down beside her. "It's not? God damn it, Claire. I don't want to leave you depressed or heartbroken. Maybe I should just forget moving to London. You need me more—"

"No, I'm not having you do that. You've been selfless enough. I'll be fine. Honestly," she broke in, shaking her head as she placed a hand on his shoulder. "It's trivial. I've been through enough break-ups, and this one is no different."

"No, this is different, sweetie. Because in this one, you actually love the guy," Darren objected as he squeezed her knee. "Look, it will work out in the end. Just don't give up."

"I know, I know. I just don't what else to do," Claire said as she exhaled and leant her head against his shoulder.

Darren patted her clasped hands. "You've just got to be persistent, baby. That's what you've got to do."

***

ZACK

Zack sat uncomfortably, twiddling his thumbs as he glanced towards the clock. His crisp white shirt felt like a second skin, and there was the need to constantly continue shifting his feet as a distraction in response to the anxiety creeping against him.

This was it.

All this hassle came down to this. The chair adjacent to him would entail him to look eye to eye with his father as he either fell to his knees in shame or stood on two feet with victory. This was his time to completely banish his father's control for once and for all.

Olivia entered the conference room, several key members of staff following. They quickly headed to take their seats around the oval-shaped table before finally the man of the hour entered. Elijah Benson. His almighty father. The man had no idea why he was sent here. *No idea at all.*

Grey suit, broad shoulders, tall manner, and highlights of silver through his once-prominent black hair. Everyone felt the atmosphere change; it didn't matter if the old man was retired. He just had that effect on everyone.

"Zack." He nodded, confidently sitting down in the chair as all attention latched onto the interaction between father and son. And there was that signature smile that both he and Jared had inherited that could light up a room in a matter of seconds.

Around the room, there was also the few key members of the board who had been invited, the exact men who were once strung with loyalty to his father but nothing money couldn't buy. No wonder they refused eye contact with the very man they'd betrayed.

And now this had to begin.

There was just no telling what his father thought. His expression was too neutral and relaxed. Even his hands rested comfortably clasped together ahead on the table in front of him. No trace of anger, frustration, or happiness; the man was completely unreadable.

Towards the end of the meeting, there were a few light discussions occurring between peers, yet Zack was anticipating his father's response. What was he going to say? Would he just sigh in disappointment? Not breathe a word and just stand up and leave? There were many options, many scenarios, but nothing could be compared to his real reaction.

Zack could see a shift physically in his father's demeanour, his back straightened as he sat up. On cue, Zack clipped his fingers, signalling Olivia to usher the rest of the members from the room to leave his old man and himself to whatever discussion was about to occur.

"Well?" Zack muttered after the last person left the room.

"Well, indeed," Elijah reiterated, exhaling lightly as he picked up the glass of water in front of him. "What would you like me to say, Zack?" He cleared his throat after taking a light sip of the water as if he were tasting expensive wine.

"What's your response? Don't go all quiet on me, Dad. Speak what you feel. You normally like to pitch a fork into everything so quickly. So…" Zack prodded, his eyebrows lifting up.

"C'mon. Don't be shy." If the patronising tone wasn't enough to tick his father off, then his father was biting down on his tongue really hard.

Elijah laughed without an ounce of humour. "Oh, son. What does it matter if I speak my mind? You've gone ahead with this monstrosity anyway, and I told you there would be consequences. It's just a disappointment, that is all—"

"And there's the father I know. But I don't think I'll have to worry about your threats," Zack interrupted, knowing he was very lucky that he wasn't a stranger to have broken into his father's point otherwise his head might have been delivered on a silver service platter.

"Zack, let's be real. I can easily take back control, and you *know* I am a man of my word on consequences," he replied, shifting his chair back.

Zack smirked.

The smirk on Zack's face vexed his father who with some attempt, humorously said. "You'll make the end to this company, Zack. Who is going to want to work with someone who hasn't got the balls to continue a capitalist affair? They don't want green nature hippies fucking them over."

Zack's smile drew into a sly nature, something that surprised his father further. "That's where you're wrong, Father. I know you were behind those projects failing. I've been undercover within the company, and I found out about all those missing funds and manipulations," Zack began, confidently brushing his fingers across the glass surface of the table. "And! Oh! Just this morning, I've received good news." He laughed lightly, eyeing his father from the corner of his eye. "Yes," he continued, staring him straight in the face. "Not even that damn magazine has come out yet, and yet…Japanese innovators want partnership with Benson's Corporations." He folded his arms as he casually leant against the table. "To support in innovating and by best means improving sustainable living as well." He shrugged his shoulders. "They must have liked what they saw. You can thank Olivia." He pointed to his secretary, who stood in the corner of the room, shyly glancing away. "She helped promote. Fished in some interest, and well…" He rocked gently forth and back. "I've got a shareholder. I wouldn't call that an end to business, would you? And that means I'll probably make more profit that you ever have."

Elijah was lost for words. He had nothing to be afraid of. And now, this was more victorious seeing his father curl into a ball, baffled and completely weakened.

"Dad." Zack frowned playfully. "You're not mad, are you? I know I must be very incompetent." Sarcasm dripped through his tone. "And I know I have no balls to do what you have so dexterously achieved." Zack sighed. "Oh, well." He pushed himself off the table. "I'll just show you out. Give my love to Mom when you get back."

His father had still not spoken a word, too stunned and stubborn to fumble a word of praise. He could only move his feet, barely heading for the door as his son followed behind. It was only when he reached the door did he turn and manage an audible sentence. "I cannot understand…"

"Never mind," Zack replied, spurring on his father to continue walking.

"How? I…" Pausing at the door of the lift, Zack dismissed his father's wild trance and pressed the button to call for the single, metal shaft. "Son, it's—"

"Disappointing, I know." He sighed, ushering his father into the lift as he stood confidently where he was. "Whatever will I do? Have a nice day, Dad." Smiling as the doors shut, he left his confused father wondering what in hell had occurred.

"Couldn't have gone better, I'd say. Don't you think?" Zack said to Olivia, who handed him his phone and belongings.

"Yes, sir, shall I—"

"Olivia, you have done more than enough. Have the day off. Thank you for your great contribution towards my one-time dilemma," he interrupted, squeezing her shoulder with his free hand as an act of encouragement and gratitude.

Now, he had only had a few more problems to solve.

***

CLAIRE

Claire was digging into a breast of chicken topped with crispy bacon and potato wedges on the side. And she was also trying to compete with the basket of sadness sitting heavily on her shoulders over her current love life.

She wasn't even really eating, just moving food about with her fork as she debated whether or not to just throw it out or that magically her appetite would just appear.

Would it hurt to try phoning Zack again?

Claire sighed, placing her fork on the side beside her untouched food as she took out her mobile phone from her jeans' pocket. Holding her breath, she dug through the contacts, deliberately disregarding the fact his number was in most recent that she had phoned, preferring that it gave her more time to debate whether it was the right thing to do and pretend she'd never phoned him in her life.

It was now or never, she thought as she pressed down on the dial button, hearing immediately the dialling tone connecting to Zack's phone. It went on, something she'd expected considering all the last had gone straight to voicemails.

She sank down in her chair, knowing the automated message would chirp in, signalling that the receiver was unavailable. Claire expected it and dreaded it.

Then suddenly, the dialling stopped, and then there was what Claire could faintly hear as steady breathing. She shot up, holding the phone close to her ear as she begged in desperation, "Zack, please don't end the call! Please." She almost imagined his finger hovering over the red telephone icon to cut their connection abruptly off. "I know I don't deserve the time of the day right now, but I need you to hear this." There was still not a word of reply, just the interference of background noises of what appeared to be late night traffic combined with his anxious state. "Zack." Holding back tears, she gripped her fingers around the fork, turning her knuckles white. "I'm sorry for what I did. It was sly. I love you, Zack, and even if I was the best goddamn actress in the world, I couldn't pull off lying to your face about how I feel. I know that. I…thought I was being selfless…but it was selfish. I was thinking about myself. You lied, yeah, and it sucked…but I know now that you hadn't lied about how you felt…at least I hope that now you still feel the same. I'm so sorry, Zack." Her voice croaked gently as she swallowed back a gulp of tears. "Don't give up on me...p-please...I-I need you." Claire was unable to stop the flow of tears as she pleaded desperately, wanting him to reply; it could have been a grunt or a sigh, anything, yet her anticipation was over when the call ended, leaving her in an emotional state with a deadline.

CHAPTER TWENTY

ZACK

"I am Zack Benson."
Ah, no.
"Well, hello folks, I am Mr. Zack Benson."
Definitely not.
"I am the CEO, Mr. Zack Benson, of Benson's Corporations."

Zack exhaled. Why on earth he was practicing his name in front of the bathroom mirror? It hadn't suddenly changed. *Bloody hell,* he thought when he completely missed following through the loop as he adjusted his dark purple tie around the collar of his white shirt. So far, he'd already washed soap in his eyes, creating a few agonising seconds where he'd also nearly slipped on the pale white bathroom tiles searching for the towel. Zack's day was not on the best start, which he knew

261

had to drastically change before he arrived at work.

Today was the day. The weekly business insider, pouring its heart out on Zack Benson, would be released, already stocked up in shops as briefed by his PA, Jay. But for those who he had worked with, they had not a clue; they camouflaged Zack. Like grass from the Savannah, they hid the hungry lion, unaware that the bigger threat was right beneath their noses.

He'd also caught glimpses, actually, no lies; he read the entire interview and the piece revolved around him. The photo they used was breathtakingly good, not in a vain way of treasuring his attractive features, but for the fact it portrayed the fearless leader that Zack begged to be. It made him feel proud that hopefully the business world would now welcome him into open arms and register that Elijah Benson was retired. It was a big deal for him.

So much shit would be uncovered.

It made him anxious. On this dismal, rainy Thursday morning, he would be burying Zack Chase six feet into the ground, jammed tightly shut with nails so the lie could never return. He'd already seen the damage caused when he revealed the truth to Claire; only he expected he'd have little to worry about considering he wasn't in romantic relations with the entire populace who worked for Benson's

Corporations.

Steadying his hands on the sink, he took a single breath in, watching as lips drew out.

Now or never.

"Kyle?" he called out as he headed downstairs into the open layout of the central living room. As far as anyone would speculate, it would seem that not a soul lived within this complex, as everything was so neat and tidy. Not an ounce of dust, no discarded rubbish left lying about, and certainly no odd knick knacks—much credit to the maid. "Have you seen my phone anywhere? I'm pretty sure I didn't leave it at work," he asked as he adjusted the right black cuff on his shirt's wrist.

He'd offered Kyle the guest room down across the hallway from Zack's after he had showed up with bottles of booze. At some point, they must have grown tired, so Kyle stayed the remainder of the night.

Out of nowhere, his friend walked up beside him with an outstretched hand holding his phone. "Here," Kyle said with a short nod. He must have only just woken up, the state of his shirt's collar stuck up and his hair bedraggled from his tangle with the bedsheets. "You left it on the side table last night…I *answered* it." He cleared his throat as his eyes quickly flicked to the floor.

"Oh, who was it?"

"Claire."

Zack slid his tongue across the bottom of his lip, tasting mint toothpaste. "*Why*?"

"Why, *what*?" Kyle replied, his brows drawing into a state of confusion. His grey socks shuffled a little on the floor as he relaxed his right hand on his hip.

"Why answer it?" Zack shook his head as he snatched his phone out of Kyle's hand.

"*Why*? Because she is *ringing* you to death. I thought you were ready to move on from all of this. Sort things out between you. Zack, you should have heard her on the phone. She was in tears. Begging. *She*—" He gave up midway because of the defeat in Zack's eyes. "Dude?" he quietly muttered, patting a hand on Zack's shoulder. "You two can't keep going on like this."

Zack shrugged off Kyle's hand from his shoulder as he slid his phone into his trouser pocket. "What's more important today is clearing my name in the office. I need people to respect me. Know that I'm the boss and...as for Claire, that can wait. So...stop." A final warning echoed through his stern tone as Zack headed over to the kitchen.

Kyle sighed lightly, kicking his bare foot into the air as if he were tapping a football gently to the next player.

Zack bit down on his tongue, glaring through the huge, double-glazed windows, rain meandering down the pane obstructing the city landscape. Part of him wished he was there when she rang, but another part was glad he didn't have to listen to her voice, afraid that her sincerity was just deception mimicking the same case as that weekend.

He had to shove it away from his thoughts, focus on getting today over and done with.

***

CLAIRE

Claire was tempted to give up. She was trying to make the decision to cut Zack off, push him away as if he didn't exist in her life, but that was terribly hard. So instead, she tried, and she did really try, to get on with her work, which was now updating a few sections of the company's website. This was the attempt to improve marketing: update the old to bring in the new. And to save her job.

Graves was up ahead doing his routine walks too, checking individuals' screens as he perched a hand on their shoulder as he leaned in. If he hadn't been doing exactly the same to the men as he was to the women, it might be construed as flirting.

"Hey." A voice startled Claire out of the blue. "Sorry," Jason apologised once she recognised it was him who had crept up behind her. "You doing all right?" He stole the empty chair beside her and sat down.

"Y-yeah," she replied timidly as she tucked a strand of hair behind her ear. "Just updating the website that Graves tasked me to do. You?"

"I'm good…" Jason muttered, scrutiny written within his eyes, suspicious of Claire's reply. "You sure you're all right?"

"Yeah, so hey, it's getting closer to meeting your girl. Nervous? I saw you posted yesterday on Facebook that it's only a week or—"

"Don't dodge the question, Claire," Jason interrupted, his eyes locking with hers. "What's up?"

"Nothing." She nervously chuckled, shaking her head. "I'm f—"

She wasn't able to finish off her sentence to convince Jason when Graves began to suddenly clap his hands, attracting the attention of the entire office. For whatever reason, it seemed important, and as the office gradually quieted down, with those returning to their seats, Claire could then make out a woman with a pair of spectacles propped on the end of her nose, meekly standing beside Graves.

"Attention—"

"That won't be necessary," a familiar voice cut in, startling Graves at the abrupt interruption. Claire's heart stopped—a second maybe, maybe three—but it stopped. She knew, even if she wasn't convinced herself, that it was

Zack, and there he was heading for the front of the office, sending those beside herself into a pool of confusion. Confidence radiated from him as if he were God's gift sent to earth.

"*Excuse* me?" Graves laughed coldly, disliking how he had been cut off. "Don't interrupt me. Get to your seat—"

"That's Mr. Benson to you," Zack coolly responded, snapping his fingers that signalled Olivia to his side. She slid a copy of what appeared to be a magazine to his hand. He didn't say a word for several seconds or so, just remained calmly quiet, an intimidating calmness that had everyone, even herself, anxious. Then he slid his free hand into his pocket whilst effortlessly balancing the magazine open on a page in the palm of his hand. "I know this may come to you as a surprise," he began. "I'm indeed the CEO of this company. No, there are no hidden cameras. This is not a program in which I've signed to go undercover and is being broadcast on Channel Four. This was done purely out of speculation on whether my company is working to the highest standards."

There were a few mutters of shock, a gasp from Jason, who was still sitting by Claire, yet she was more concerned with trying to get Zack to at least look her way. A look, a wink, or some expression to show that he had heard her last night, forgiven her, despised her if it came to it, just something to show that he had been there. He refused to look over, his eyes staying stubbornly focused on everyone except her.

"I must confess," he continued, his eyes scanning the room. "I have mixed feelings. Some of you pleasantly surprised me, and others…" Claire wondered if that implied her. "…were a disappointment." Then he paused, a hushed silence around the room. "*Graves!*" He snapped his fingers as he turned his head over his right shoulder, ushering the man forward, who was still shocked by the revelation. "Come here and look at this." He held the magazine out and watched with some glint of humour in his eyes as Graves weakly took it. "Is *that* not me?"

"N—I mean, yes, it is you," Graves mumbled, not as hot on the wheels as he usually was when in the spotlight of the entire office. Instead, he seemed shy as a mouse, gobsmacked evidently. As Zack turned to talk with the rest of them, Graves' eyes flicked back and forth hurriedly from the magazine to Zack.

Zack's smile broadened as he said nothing for a moment before he snapped, causing a few up the front of the office to jump as he barked. "Graves, you're fired!" He clasped his hands excitedly before patting the man's shoulder. "Pack your things and get out of my building. You've conspired against this company, and your behaviour will not be tolerated here."

Again, there was another chorus of gasps

around the room. If Claire didn't hate the man, she might have felt some sympathy for him, but this was the man who treated his staff with disrespect, was suspected of selling steroids right on the company's doorstep, as well as using some funding for his own expense.

"W-what? But, sir! What did I do wrong? I don't understand," Graves shrilled, panicking as he tried to reason with the man who was paying no attention to him at that moment.

"Mr. Graves, do not embarrass yourself any further," Zack replied, shunning him as he then motioned two men over she had not noticed till now to escort Mr. Graves from the premises.

"As for the rest of you…continue with the great work. Under inspection, and hearing from some of your opinions, I'm creating a system to make it easier for those with younger children who are unable to get childcare, and I am increasing wages to reward your hard work. More discussion of these changes will be planned." From the corner of the room, Zack nodded respectfully towards a woman who held a grateful smile against her lips. It was a promise he had made himself to ensure he could help those who had given real feedback for working at the company. "Now as for who will be taking over this department, I'm granting this to Miss Claire Winter." He gave a confident nod but still refused to meet her eyes.

Oblivious to those clapping, she was only

woken from her despair when Jason patted her shoulder, smiling and congratulating her.

"As for the latest project, I'm recruiting a small team within this department, and the same will be made through all other departments to work on pushing this sustainable attitude forward," Zack continued, drawing all attention back to the front.

"I want to thank each and every one of you for your work under Benson's Corporations. I can see that this company works at its fullest capacity to ensure work is done correctly. Feel free to relax for the remainder of the day and pick up a magazine with yours truly featured. Again, thank you." He nodded, his hands spreading out as if he were about to cuddle each and every of one into his arms.

Then the eruption of clapping happened; it seemed apparent that each and every one of them looked up to him and were notably impressed. Even Jason, who once might have despised the man with their earliest collision, had a look of admiration. And there was Zack looking pleased at the front, welcoming those who dared to get up and offer a hand to shake, thanking him.

But even though she had heard her name from his lips, his eyes didn't twitch towards her, and that made her stomach walls clench. Hadn't any of those words she said last night meant a thing?

"Can you believe this?" Jason gasped, grabbing Claire's attention as the rest of the office shuffled off into conversation. "That guy!" He jabbed his finger to the front. "Was the fucking boss all this while? My god! What a man!" Laughing, he clapped his hands again with surprise.

Amongst the office, she could also hear those voicing their own opinions on the matter.

"That's the CEO? God, I can't believe he was right in our office all this while!"

"Wage increases? Fuck yeah."

"I sat next to that guy."

"I had the hots for him. Boy, imagine if we were together."

"Thank god, he got rid of Graves! Too bad Monica left. He would have had a dig at her."

Claire sighed, feeling utterly vulnerable and certainly left out. If she hadn't known Zack, hadn't encountered him, and never put that ad up for a potential roommate, she might have shared the exact same feelings, content that some powerful man was making positive changes around the office.

"Wait, Claire, you were living with the CEO!" Jason blurted out, slapping a hand against his cheek as he chuckled. "And this was…the guy who—man, mind blown!"

At the front, she could see Zack discussing with several people surrounding him before finally it appeared it was time for him to make an exit. At a loss, her mouth gaped as she watched him leave, Olivia beside him, hurrying to keep up with his stride. As far as her promotion came, she wasn't entirely fixed into the position till further notice, so as far as she could see, the rest of the day wouldn't need her attention.

Getting to her feet, she ignored Jason's query as she pushed her chair away and headed down the aisle, heading for the lifts. On her way, she was greeted with words of congratulations, pats on the back, and smiles before they returned to their erratic discussion on today's revelation.

Pushing past all of this, she reached the lift, pressing the button desperately more than once as she caught a surge of adrenaline with the need to find Zack immediately. Shuffling in, she pressed firmly onto the control pad to shut the metallic doors, hoping they'd comply quickly.

Out of sheer desperation as soon as the doors opened to the reception of the establishment, she ran out, giving no thought that she might be bombarded with the rush hour of those returning from lunch. As she suspected, she was and made no apology as she pushed past a fairly plump man, who blabbered a few words of profanity at her abrupt shove aside.

The doors were ahead, and she caught sight of a dark, bulky SUV parked momentarily before it drove away from the curb. Zack was in there. Claire just knew it.

Crying out with protest, she yelled his name at the foot of the curb, drawing attention as she stood, holding her head in her hands with vexation.

"Shit, shit," she cried, biting down on her tongue as she paced around in a small semi-circle of space.

"*Claire*?"

She turned, panting as she dragged her hands through her hair. "Do I know you?" she asked, her expression painted still with anguish.

"I'm...Kyle, Zack's friend," Kyle meekly said, angling his head to the side warily as he held his free hand that wasn't holding the cup of coffee out as if he were petting a frightened bear cub.

"Where is he going?" she blurted out, pointing to the empty space that had held the SUV.

Kyle parted his lips gently, then he said, "Zack hasn't spoken to you?"

"No, no." Claire shook her head, unable to keep still on the spot. "Where is he going? He can't just leave like that. I need to speak to him! He—" Her breathless plea was cut off by Kyle's comforting hand on her shoulder.

"Whoa, whoa. Zack's got a sudden business trip to Japan," he said, his words feeling like a tsunami hitting her flat in the face.

"What?"

"Yeah…I thought that you two might have—
"

"I need to see him! I have to get to the airport!" she cried out, desperately racing back to the curb as she scanned for a black cab.

Kyle placed his coffee on a nearby bench, drawing up to Claire's side as he registered her emotional state. "I'll take you," he offered, scooping out his car keys from his trouser pocket. "Come on." They raced to his car.

One more chance. One more chance.

CHAPTER
TWENTY-ONE

The scent of sterile, pinewood disinfectant stung Zack's nostrils as he casually skimmed his eyes across the depressing horizon with the onset of the afternoon sun in the background shining over the planes.

He wasn't as tied up as other travelling passengers who had to rely on the airlines to prep the plane for flight…no, Zack was fortunate that he could request an immediate private small jet at any accessible airport. The only delay he had to experience was the transfer of his luggage and the exclusive, dodge-the-queue security checks.

Zack exhaled, his elbows resting on his thighs with his hands clasped in between the centre of his legs, and with the dreary expression superglued to the stretch of his face, he looked quite drastically different to the intimidating man he was a few hours ago. You would have thought he would have been happy, proud that he had made changes to his business. You would have thought he'd be satisfied that he could promote Claire to the position he knew she had only dreamed of. But he wasn't happy. No, he was fed up.

The man who would have looked forward to the several hours in flight accompanied with the hot air hostess, three course meals, and a healthy glass of champagne was petrified. Had been since that attack of the warm, fuzzy feeling that powered the fear that if he ever lost it, he would become a crippling mess entangled in a deep, black hole unable to escape. Perhaps that was a little dramatic, but for a man who had fallen in love for the first time, he was every inch vulnerable.

"Sir." One of the airline attendants smiled as she passed him his passport. "Everything is on the green light. We're just doing our routine checks and then you'll be set to head off," she explained, flashing her dazzling set of pearly whites followed with her deep, red lipstick that any other day Zack would have been quick to flirt with her.

He cleared his throat, taking his passport from her hand. "Thank you." Just a polite nod as he shuffled back into the leather chair. Surrounding him, he could hear the odd flutes of champagne, pink prosecco, or merely apple or orange juice clink from whatever occasion these affluent travellers were celebrating.

Zack had already stumbled upon the magazine, neatly situated on the end corner table. In big, bold print, it read his name, and on pages four to five, there rested his picture and the short interview conducted, along with background information. He couldn't stand the sight of it, so he already had tucked it under some brochure on some airline's extravagant deals on trips to Dubai that ticked the prices of above £3,000 per passenger and that was only for the plane ticket.

If things didn't fix themselves, then perhaps he could see this as a learning curve, refuse to fall in love again or attempt to go back to his old, boisterous ways. Either way, he was hoping that wouldn't be the case. Part of him felt utterly stupid for leaving like that, a coward to stand up to his fears and talk things out. Yet he'd tried that. And twice, perhaps even three times, she wasn't having it. And then when that weekend happened, it really destroyed him. Zack knew that. He couldn't understand how someone who was supposed to love him would avenge what he mistakenly did, to break his heart and make him feel as disposable as a packet of crisps thrown on the pavement. He hated that feeling. Hated feeling like he wasn't worth the time and, in that context, just a quick fuck to make someone else feel better. It broke his confidence. And because of that, here he was, stubborn as all mighty and reluctant to give it another shot because of the fear that it could further shatter him.

Maybe part of him was already trying to move on. Just moments before he arrived in the VIP room, he finally got around to deleting her unheard voicemails one after the other. Perhaps Zack had already given up or he was just scared.

Picking up his glass of water, he swallowed the liquid, feeling as if he were suddenly intaking a bowl of cement down his neck. It was just fucking him up.

From the distance, even despite the classical music playing softly in the background of the room, he could hear the alerting late passengers to board some flight to New York that they should have boarded thirty minutes ago.

It was a comfort being in an airport. Zack could always remember and would experience the exact feeling of excitement fill the walls of his lungs and stomach. There just wasn't anything better than being dropped off at an airport and knowing in a matter of several hours you could be on the way to some other part of the world. It was a lot easier for Zack to travel when he was a kid; money didn't come short nor did the exotic destinations. No matter how many times he was tucked up in that seat staring anxiously out the small window, thrilled with the small tiny, visible, orange jacketed men at dawn or dusk carrying out their safety checks, he'd always have that same feeling—the one that felt like eating a well-made meal. As a grown man, it became at times less and less, used to exploring the elite décor, fed gourmet food and in-flight comfort, because for a man who could buy a ticket anytime for anywhere around the world, it became lonely and the same old.

***

KYLE

Kyle didn't even need to pick out his car as already Claire was hurrying to the side of his grey sports convertible, desperately holding onto the handle. Getting into the driver's seat, Kyle shoved in the key, permitting the engine to roar to life as from the corner of his eyes, he could see Claire anxiously fastening her seatbelt. He could hear her sniffling, dry tears against her cheeks, deepening the guilt he felt for his part to play in all of this.

He gave a little juice to the pedal, and the car rocked into motion, heading to the surface from the underground parking. "Claire," he began warily. "I'm sorry about all this shit. I feel bad.

If I hadn't—"

***

CLAIRE

"None of this is your fault, Kyle," she weakly said, saddened to hear her hoarse, slightly raspy voice. "We're *just* two stubborn people scared to commit...I never intended to fall in love with Zack, and nor did he." She pushed back a flyaway behind her ear as she focused her attention on the road.

Kyle offered a sympathetic smile. "We'll get there, Claire. I promise I'll get you there."

Claire registered his sincerity. "Thank you."

Outside was another picture. They hadn't even passed work as they were stuck in lunch hour traffic, also accompanied with the few patches of roadwork going on. It just didn't seem at all hopeful for Claire as she quietly squeezed her eyes, hoping that when she opened them, she'd be in Zack's arms or at least breathing in the same room as him.

Kyle could see her distress, so he turned off the radio that he only realised was playing in the background. All they could hear and see was the wash of the wiper blades consistently sliding back and forth at the slow downfall of rain. Way to make a person feel any better,

Kyle thought as he glimpsed at the dark, stormy grey skies. His father always used to tell him as a kid, grey skies was God having a shower—not that they were religious, but it just always was the way.

"I know this isn't…going to make you feel any better, or maybe it will, but Zack does…love you, Claire," Kyle comforted, slowing the car as the brake lights from the car ahead piped on. "He's…a right mess without you."

Claire nodded, still with a saddened expression but no words.

"I'm also sorry to hear about your friend's boyfriend. I know Zack seemed brave about it all, but it sucked for him. How is your…friend?" Kyle asked, not knowing if speaking was the right thing to do, but he couldn't help it; he just had the need to talk when he got a little too jumpy.

She swallowed. "Thank you," she muttered, pausing before answering his question. "He's moving to London. He needs a fresh start, and it's…where J-Jonas…got his promotion and where they were going to move, *so* Darren has gone to follow their dream." Another sad thought that she wouldn't see her friend daily.

"He'll be…fine," Kyle muttered, unsure if his reassurance sounded weak. "And…so will you."

Claire looked down to her cold, numb hands.

"I just hope it's not too late."

"It won't be."

"I really...hope so."

Kyle crossed over the main road heading out of the city, following the signs that suddenly appeared giving them en route to the city's airport.

There was once this one story that Claire had read. It was one of those stories that left you with an open ending, left to your interpretation. Some hated those type of endings, the ones where it left you without a happy ending or sad but made it so you should have to think, dwell on it for weeks to come, wondering whatever happened to those characters. Did they make it? Did it cruelly go wrong for them?

This one she read was quite different, nothing cliché with the married life, kids, and flashing lights in romance novels in the end. Instead, the couple who had went through everything lost everything and attempted to fix it; there was no ending line to prove if it was ever resolved.

In the end, on the train platform where they promised to meet, the man standing nervously biting his nails, red scarf whipping in his face from the autumn chill, popped to the toilets, thus missing the train. The girl who was anxiously glancing out the train window saw his figure walking away, a thought popping into her mind that he didn't want this, and so she remained on the train, and when he returned, she wasn't on the platform waiting for him. So an open ending. It made Claire ponder for nights on end, wondering if they found each other, one rang up and the mistake was resolved. Whether they had the kids, marriage, or home?

Love is unpredictable.

Kyle was hitting the forties now as he accelerated down the long road that was heading onto the motorway. They hadn't spoken for the last ten minutes; Claire was fidgeting more by the second and holding that same sombre look.

Above already, she could see a huge double decker and single planes passing over, taking flight to another world, another time and place, whilst others could be landing.

The rain had also stopped, and the clouds were less dark than they were back in the central city.

"I really hope he's here," Claire muttered, squeezing the palms of her hands together as she closed her eyes. Kyle was heading into the terminal for international flights. Already, he could see the odd taxi filing out passengers who were collecting their suitcases. A little girl with ponytails and a pink rabbit in her hand joyfully pushed her tiny suitcase around as her parents dished across the cash for payment. And then as they as they passed them, it was like a movie scene seeing another emotional scene of a young adult hugging his distressed mother who was watching her brave boy head off into the world.

Claire was unfastening her seatbelt, sitting up more eagerly as she scanned the terminal platform, wondering if perhaps she would see Zack. *"Where are you? Where are you?"* she muttered frantically.

"I'll park us in the short stay," Kyle said, turning right and heading away from the airport, causing a gasp in her throat. "Then if I'm correct, Zack should be…I mean will be in the VIP boarding rooms. *Okay?"*

She nodded several times, sitting back as she inhaled and exhaled, almost panting as she dug her nails into her palms.

Kyle parked the car. Getting quickly out, he locked the car then hurried after Claire. "Claire! Wait!" he called after her, finding himself suddenly in a chase as she ran back the way they came.

Claire wasn't even thinking straight as she raced to the revolving doors where departures were heading off to their sunny destinations. "Claire!" She heard her name several times more, but she refused to slow down. The stair escalators were just ahead, destined for the second floor where it would bring people towards their check-ins.

She dodged past people, choosing the stairs

instead as she climbed them rapidly, forgetting that even as she reached the second floor, she had no clue where she was going and was left in a heated maze of travellers pulling along suitcases and others heading straight onto security checks.

"Claire!" Kyle panted, hunching his back over. "Slow down! I need to catch—"

"I'm sorry," she apologised, feeling guilty for heading off like that. Resting her hand on his back, she allowed him to breathe and just for that moment ignored that twitching feeling telling her to race off. "Do you know where he'll be?"

Kyle exhaled, standing up. "Yes, maybe. But we won't be able to access some parts as we're required to actually be paying travellers…but…" Exhaling once more, he brushed back some sweat from his forehead. "I know a shortcut."

Claire nodded, this time walking as she followed Kyle, who headed to where all the duty-free, restaurants, and bars were stacked in the centre of the airport. Already, she felt like she was seeing things, odd men who had the thick, black mop of hair that churned anxiety through her stomach.

"I have a pass, which means I can get to the VIP. I'm a regular flyer, so they might let me even if I'm not intending to fly today, which I hope is not the case," Kyle joked, taking a right turn. "But I know he hasn't left yet."

Claire nodded, absent-minded as she took in the sight of crowds of people passing by.

Kyle stopped at a door; a golden plaque adjacent said it was exclusive for its affluent flyers. Walking in, he stopped at the desk where a ginger-haired attendant smiled, suspicious by their flustered state.

"Can I help you, sir? This is for our exclusive guests. Checks in are also back that way along with the security—"

"I have a pass," he cut her off, pulling out his wallet from his back pocket as he frantically searched for the membership. "Look." He focused on his wallet. "I need to reach my friend, who is heading off to Japan. Zack Benson. I'm Kyle Wickes, a friend, and this is…" He paused as he pondered what was appropriate to Claire's status, "…his girlfriend. I have no flight booked, but it's important that I get to him." He slid the card alongside his driver's licence for ID.

"I'm sorry, sir." She smiled politely. "But we don't usually allow even our customers to enter without—"

"Look…" He paused as he quickly read her name tag. "*Jenny*, right? I need to get in there. This is a crisis. I'm a paying VIP, and I can promise I have no intention to sneak onto a plane. I just want to see my friend."

"Sir—"

"Money? How much? I'm willing to pay. Just please, Jenny, let me see Mr. Benson," Kyle begged, tapping his finger against the desk.

The attendant's smile deflated a little. "I—"

"Please," Kyle said once more.

Her lips gaped open a little before she nodded. "Okay, but I'll have to let Mr. Benson know first. Your name, Kyle Wickes, correct?"

Kyle nodded. "Yes, just say his friend needs to urgently see him."

The attendant nodded before slipping away through the double, purple-tinted doors.

"Thank you, Kyle," Claire said, grasping his hand as she squeezed it tight. "Thank you, thank you."

Kyle blushed. "You're welcome."

It must have only been three seconds later, and Jenny the attendant returned, nodding. "Yes, you can enter. Mr. Benson is sitting straight ahead."

Kyle thanked her then turned to Claire. "It's best if you go in alone. I'll wait here with Jenny." He briefly flicking his eyes to the woman who was standing behind the desk, vaguely more interested in the conversation than her computer screen. "*Just*…fix it." He squeezed his hand on her shoulder as Claire nodded.

Then inhaling, she headed for the doors, pushing them lightly as the circulation around her body intensified and all she could hear even over the clatter of conversation was her heart thumping like a drum.

You can do this, she thought. *You can do this*.

No one really took much interest as she entered, even if her work clothes were a little wrinkled and her messy ponytail had flyaways. Most stuck to their own business, laughing at jokes or ordering small beverages at the bar.

Inside, it was fairly dim, the creation of a casual, elegant atmosphere erected from the small, round spotlights on the floor and the purple lampshades above the bar stools. Claire glanced around meekly, afraid that the attendant had got it all wrong, mixed up Zack Benson with a stranger, and the man she loved was already halfway across the world to Japan.

Each stranger she encountered escalated her fear, churned her stomach inside out, and if she was going to faint, she hoped she would at least land on that comfortable-looking brown sofa than the wooden floor.

And then she stopped.

Zack.

There he was.

Sitting with his back towards her as he held a glass of water in his hand as he casually looked outside.

What was she going to say? How on earth? God, her insides were on fire.

"*Fuck,*" she whispered to herself.

Claire had never felt so frightened in her life. It was like meeting him for the first time. Some blind date. A headteacher's visit in primary school. The judge with his final verdict. Kissing your crush for the first time.

And here she was, suddenly picturing the first smirk, their first encounter when he stood all mysterious outside work. Darren beside her, telling her to hastily message him back, wondering if that was him.

The nicknames, their bickering, the sex, and just his mere presence.

Fuck, they had been through so much.

Taking a deep, nerve-wrecking breath, she slowly made her way over. From the side, he looked so lost, transfixed, so he didn't even notice when she sat down beside him in the adjacent leather chair.

God, she was right near him. She could smell that familiar musky cologne, picture those hands holding tight on her, and even remember that small tattoo on his hip from his drunken mistake.

Just do it, she thought.

Taking another slow breath, she turned gently towards him as she found herself saying words. "Hello…my name is Claire Winter." Her voice tuned him into reality as he looked at her with shock. His brows lifted, and his lips gaped a little open, gobsmacked as she could tell by the sight of her sitting there. She didn't give him chance to speak. "I'm twenty-four..." Swallowing, she kept her composure, feeling exposed under his staring eyes. "My favourite colour is grey, and I could eat BBQ ribs all day without a doubt. I'm...caring..." Her right shoulder subconsciously lifted up. "Friendly, and confident...but I can be stubborn and sometimes spiteful." Then she looked down briefly before returning her eyes to his bewitched ones. "I've just recently went...through a *terrible*...break-up. I hurt someone I love. Like really *hurt* them and...I don't know if we'll ever go back to how things used to be, but...no matter what, I'll always love them and be there for them." Holding back the tears she felt, Claire swallowed another mouthful of air. "I know your name is Zack Benson. You're...funnily enough, my boss. Your favourite colour is purple...and you suck at washing up. You always...leave the toilet seat up, and you think it's funny when I get mad. You're caring, cool, and dare I say incredibly handsome in every way..." Pausing, she stopped her fingers from madly twitching in her lap. "Although *sometimes* you lie. But...you never have really. You've always been hundred percent truthful. And that's why you're...incredible." Stopping again, she looked elsewhere for a second before returning. "You've been through a lot with someone. You were there when she pretended to like some guy because she was a fool in thinking she didn't love you. You were there when her friend's boyfriend died. You danced with her at her brother's wedding, and you've plenty of times had *crazy* sex. Point is, you've always been there." Then she pressed her lips together, studying how he had not once moved. "I…would like to get to know you more. It's a little strange, I know. I'm your employee, but I really like you. I might even be crazy to dare say I love you, but Mr. Benson…" She held out a hand to shake. "I would love it if you would go on a date with me. What do you say?"

They said it took five seconds to look someone in the eye and fall in love. You're on the same wavelength. You'd do anything for that person. And faithful no matter what. It's something that could be abused in its lifetime, taken for granted, or torn to pieces. But no matter, it couldn't be helped. You couldn't help but fall in love. It suddenly latched on to you and wouldn't let go. There's no manual about it. Nothing to teach you about it. It just happened, and you'd know the second you looked someone in the eyes and spoke those simple three words, "I love you."

Ahead of her, Zack was quiet. He had not shifted a muscle. She was certain he had not blinked, either. Not even registered that her hand that she held out trembled frantically before slowly deflating and returning to her lap.

Part of her hoped he would have spoken by now…kissed her or held her tight.

Claire's stomach was clenching fiercely as she anticipated his answer. There was nothing else she could have said; she had said the entire truth. Surely, they could have a fresh start? They deserved that.

Zack then suddenly licked his bottom lip, turned his head to the front as he dropped his elbows onto the edge of his knees, and stooped his head down in between his legs towards the floor. From her perspective, it looked like a sign of defeat, suggesting that it wasn't enough for Zack.

Claire was going to get up, leave, and accept with mutual respect that perhaps it just wasn't meant to be. But then at a glimpse of his lips, the right edge of his lip that faced her, all at once, gradually curved up.

Was that a smile?

"What am I going to bloody do with you, Claire, huh?" Angling his head slightly towards her, it looked like a genuine look of relief had hugged his face. "You say you're *my* employee? *Well*, that is a problem." Then his hand snaked over and clasped to squeeze her hand. "I hope you can manage a long-haul flight."

THE END

Acknowledgements

So, here we are! The last book in the series. There are several people that I would like to acknowledge for their support in the series Boss Undercover.

I would first like to make an acknowledgment to Limitless Publishing for giving me the opportunity to publish my work. I didn't expect anything when I first sent off that manuscript—to be honest, I expected them to send back a "rejection" email, so, of course, it was a surprise and a half. They gave me a chance, and I am nothing but thankful that they've published me.

I would also like to acknowledge my editor, Toni, who has been nothing but helpful and supportive throughout the journey of these books. She has helped me really challenge myself to improve my story and has been there anytime I needed support on an idea. So, thank you, Toni. I really do appreciate what you've done.

I would like to thank my loving family and friends who constantly provide me unconditional support. It makes me feel good that I can make them proud—that's all I ever want to achieve.

I would also like to acknowledge my fans on Wattpad—where it all started. Without your support, I wouldn't be publishing this story. Your support through commenting, voting, and just in general reading the book is staggering! I appreciate it so much.

I would like to acknowledge the person who is reading this book. Thank you. You don't understand how much it means for me to think that there is someone out there who is enjoying my work.

So, thank you. I hope you enjoyed reading Boss Undercover.

About the Author

Romance is just one thing J.S.Badham cannot get enough of! Whether it's the typical cliché love-at-first-sight or I-hate-you-but-also-love-you compelling stories, they're always close to her heart! Most will probably see it as trash literature but love is what makes the world go around! So, why not romance?

Her spark for writing began at the age of fifteen; a passion ignited thanks to her favourite author, Rachel Caine (Morganville Vampires) encouraging her that writing is the ability to be able to share inner stories and connect to the world.

J.S. Badham's journey began on Wattpad, her path continues to grow, she continues to learn hoping that some day she'll share a story that is inspiring.

Social Media Links

Facebook:
https://www.facebook.com/JSBadham-146220769420998/

Twitter:
https://twitter.com/JSBADHAM1

Wattpad:
https://www.wattpad.com/user/Vampirefangsrules

Instagram:
https://www.instagram.com/j.s.badham/

Join our Reader Group on Facebook and don't miss out on meeting our authors and entering epic giveaways!

Limitless Reading

Where reading a book
is your first step to becoming

limitless...

LIMITLESS ▽ PUBLISHING *Reader Group*

Join today! *"Where reading a book is your first step to becoming limitless..."*

https://www.facebook.com/groups/LimitlessReading/